THE TENTH WARD

RANDOLPH CASEY HORROR THRILLERS
BOOK 1

ROCKWELL SCOTT

THE TENTH WARD

PROLOGUE

Although his heart was still beating, Thomas Mowry considered himself dead.

Why shouldn't he? With what the doctors had told him and his parents three days ago, there was no point sucking up any more clean air.

There had been tears and wailing and hysterics from everyone except Thomas himself. He only sat and listened to his mom, dad, and sister cry their eyes out. He'd run out of tears long ago.

Sixteen years old and no longer able to cry. Sixteen and dying.

"How are you feeling?" Thomas's mother asked him for the fifth time that day.

"I think I'll go to the cafeteria." He hopped out of bed, grabbed his portable oxygen, and left the hospital room before she said anything else.

Lunchtime was nearing, so there were a myriad of smells wafting about. Fried food, sweet desserts, and something spicy coming from the international counter.

Thomas took a plastic container of his favorite chocolate pudding and brought it to the register, where Mrs. Eloise was balancing the cash drawer before the midday rush.

She looked at him from over her glasses. "You're going to spoil your lunch, Thomas."

"Don't worry, I can always eat more."

She smirked as she pushed the drawer closed with her hip and rang him up. Thomas paid with his quick swipe card, which only employees used, but he'd managed to get one because he was there so often. "Have a good afternoon," Mrs. Eloise said.

"You too."

It was nice to have a casual conversation with someone who didn't know he was dying. She was the cafeteria manager, so she would not have heard the latest news of his prognosis.

He walked down the hallway, wishing he could eat the pudding as he went, but he needed his spare hand to pull the oxygen cylinder behind him.

He passed by the chapel and spotted Father Calvin outside. Thomas wished he'd gone the back way and used the other set of elevators.

The priest gave him a look, one that told Thomas he'd heard the news. "How are you, Thomas?"

"Fine. And you?"

Father Calvin licked his lips. "I haven't seen you here in a few weeks."

"What's the point?"

"I understand things are hard for you right now. But this is the *most* important time to have faith."

"You know I lost that long ago."

"I think you are just having a period of struggling.

Please come and attend services. I've been praying for you."

"Thanks, but obviously it didn't help."

Thomas saw that Father Calvin was sad, and that made him feel guilty. But Thomas was also disappointed about all the time he spent believing in and praying to a God who seemingly wasn't there at all. And if God was there, then clearly he hadn't cared much about Thomas to begin with.

So, Thomas grabbed the handle of his portable oxygen and walked away before Father Calvin moaned any more about his lost little sheep.

Back in his room, he ate the pudding at his desk while surfing the internet. Out of the corner of his eye, he noticed his mother watching him, and he knew she was about to say something, so he put on his headphones and cranked up some loud heavy metal music.

The chirping notification of an incoming video call interrupted the music.

Georgia.

Thomas sucked on the chocolate-covered spoon as the app danced on his screen, beckoning him to answer.

He clicked the red button and the music resumed.

He read a new article announcing the upcoming album from one of his favorite hard rock bands that he would not be around to check out.

The video-calling app chimed. He had a message.

Why are you ignoring me? Please talk :(

Thomas sighed. He clicked the messages and stared at them for a while, wondering if he should reply. Georgia could see he'd read the messages, but regardless, he closed his computer.

That was it. He had to do something.

He had to know for sure what would happen to him. No more of this guessing by the doctors or "hoping for the best" from his parents. He needed real, concrete answers.

And he only had one idea of how to get them.

———

THOMAS RARELY VISITED the game room at the end of the hall. St. Mary's, having the largest children's ward in the city, meant it was often packed with the youngest patients, so the room was noisy and, honestly, a bit depressing.

He was sixteen, and even though technically still eligible for the children's ward, still felt like he didn't belong.

He pulled his tank behind him. This particular holder had a gimpy wheel that made it wobble. The oxygen filled his nostrils first, and then his lungs, but it still couldn't stop his violent coughing fits.

As he walked to the board game closet, he caught eyes with Kristen, one of the high school volunteers. She was playing chess with Morgan, an eight-year-old, although it didn't look like they were strictly following the rules. Kristen gave him a small, awkward smile that Thomas returned. A month ago he'd asked her out to the movies. She'd shuffled her feet and looked at the ground before reluctantly agreeing. The next day, she'd told him she had plans, and they'd never rescheduled. Maybe she thought his oxygen tank or heavy wheezing would make too much noise. More likely, she wanted to go on a date with a normal boy. Thomas was only a little bit mad about it.

Besides, it was a blessing in disguise. He hadn't realized it at the time, but there was no point in starting a new relationship now.

He went into the board game closet and closed the door behind him just enough to not block out all the light. The bulb inside was dead, and no one had bothered to replace it. Nurse Donna was always going on about budget cuts.

At the back of the closet, Thomas rifled through all the old games shoved into the corner, the ones with torn boxes and missing pieces.

There, underneath them all, was what he'd been looking for. A Ouija board. Just as Georgia had said.

"Weird something like that's in there," she'd told him a week before. "Since this place is so Catholic and all. I bet if they knew they would throw it away."

"Did you tell someone about it?" Thomas had asked her.

"No." Although they'd been speaking via video chat—hospital rules—Georgia still picked up on his interest. "Why? You want to try it out? Those things are bad, you know."

"Nah," Thomas had said, waving his hand.

He hadn't mentioned his plan. She would've gotten mad at him.

Thomas blew off the layer of dust and examined it. The picture of the kids on the cover looked to be from the '80s.

What do I have to lose?

The answer was nothing. So he left the board game

closet, making sure Kristen or anyone else hadn't noticed he slipped out with the box tucked under his arm.

———

THAT NIGHT, Thomas waited until lights out—nine o'clock—before opening his door a crack and peering down the long, tiled corridor. He looked left and right, making sure no one was coming. It was after hours and past bedtime.

If he got caught, his plan would be interrupted.

He closed the heavy wooden door. It did not lock from the inside. Hospital policy.

He'd told his parents he wanted to sleep alone that night. Given his current condition, they were reluctant to leave his side, but they were usually good at giving him his privacy when he asked. They'd said they would return first thing in the morning, and he agreed.

Thomas threw the blanket off his bed. Hidden underneath was the Ouija board.

Loud thunder boomed outside. Rain pelted the window and the hard wind blew against the glass, making it shudder. Whenever the lightning struck, the dark room lit up blue.

He laid the board out on the floor and placed the planchette in the middle.

Knocking.

He pushed the entire thing under his bed just before the door opened. It was Ms. Donna, one of the regular night shift nurses. A nice woman, but if she found the Ouija board, he would be screwed. Thomas knew she was quite devout.

Ms. Donna frowned and put her hands on her hips. "Thomas, what are you doing? You should be asleep."

"I know," the boy said, pretending to be ashamed of himself. "I'll go now."

Ms. Donna forced a smile. Thomas recognized that look. He'd gotten it from all the other nurses who had access to his chart. "You need to rest. Don't you want to get out of here?"

And come right back in a few months? I don't even have that long left. What's the point?

"I'll see you tomorrow for my next shift."

"Good night, Ms. Donna." He feigned his most innocent and compliant voice.

Once the coast was clear again, Thomas took the board out from under his bed and put the planchette back in place.

He sat on the floor and looked down at the array of letters and numbers, a nervous feeling sprouting in his stomach. Although he'd planned it all day long, he was uneasy about the outcome.

"Dear God. Are you listening?" he asked out loud. He stared at the planchette, daring it to move.

It stayed still.

"Did you hear me, God? Are you there?"

He gave the little piece of plastic enough time to act, but nothing happened.

Thomas felt silly. The picture on the box showed more than one person touching the planchette, so maybe that was what caused it to work. But if God was as powerful and all-knowing as Father Calvin always talked about in the chapel, then surely he could nudge a small little board game piece on his own.

"Dear God. You know I stopped believing in you a long time ago. But I figured it was time to give you another chance. So this is your last shot to convince me you're real. Are you here right now?"

He let a long minute of silence go by. He finally released the breath he hadn't realized he'd been holding. Then, as he leaned over to pick up the board and put it away forever, the planchette moved.

It zipped over to YES.

Thomas gasped and stumbled back a few paces, startled. Yes, he had definitely seen it happen. That thing had been in the center of the board, and then moved all by itself.

His breathing quickened. His heart pounded. Thunder roared outside, sounding as if it were right on top of the hospital.

Was he in the presence of God?

Strange. He didn't feel any different. He would've thought being close to the Lord would have caused something out of the ordinary. At least, Father Calvin always made him think so.

However, the room had suddenly grown freezing.

"Who are you?" the boy asked the board.

The planchette moved again, this time darting between the letters.

GOD was spelled out.

"If you're God, tell me my name."

THOMAS

"How old am I?"

16

He backed away from the board as far as he could go, pressed against the wall, not sure if he was frightened or in awe. These were the kinds of supernatural things that Father Calvin talked about. Although he wondered why normal prayer had always resulted in silence.

Maybe Father Calvin should be using a Ouija board to get in touch with God.

"If you're real, then thank you for proving it. I struggle to believe in you sometimes."

The planchette moved again.

I FORGIVE YOU

"I'm afraid, God. They say I don't have much time left and I don't want to leave my friend Georgia behind. Do you know her? She doesn't deserve to be sick. Why are you doing this to us?"

I WILL PROTECT HER

"Do you promise?"

YES

Tears welled up in the boy's eyes. That was all he needed. If he couldn't live, then he just wanted Georgia to be okay. She was a special girl, and he was lucky to have met her, even though their time together had been short.

The next question came to his mind, but he was hesitant to ask. God could know the answer that his entire team of doctors and nurses had been looking for. It had caused him to live each day in uncertainty, walking an agonizing path of confusion and dread.

But his curiosity got the better of him.

"Do you know when I'm going to die?"

At first the planchette didn't move, but then it sprung into action.

17 DAYS

Tears flowed freely down his cheeks now. Such a short time.

But at least he knew.

And if he saw day eighteen, he would be certain God was not real. Or if he was, then he definitely wasn't all-knowing like Father Calvin said.

So, Thomas put the Ouija board back in the box and returned it under his bed sheet.

He climbed into bed and turned out the light. But with the storm booming outside and the sudden foreknowledge of his fate, Thomas found it very difficult to get to sleep.

1

Randolph Casey held up three fingers.

"How many fingers do you see?"

The room was much too large for his class, which made it look sparsely attended even on a good day. Since it was the Friday before a big football game, and the middle of the afternoon, nearly half of his students had flaked.

"Three," someone answered.

"Good." Rand brought his hand down. "Today's lesson will be all about the number three." He clicked the space bar on his computer and the PowerPoint presentation began. The first slide was a big 3 he'd taken from the internet. "Can anyone tell me why this number is important for our purposes?"

He paced in front of the front row of students. The seating was stadium-style, like a movie theater. Each student had two or three desks between them—except the ones who were close friends.

"It's the time this class starts?"

Rand didn't catch who said it, but it received a fair share of chuckling from the other students, as well as Rand himself.

"True," he said, a smile on his face, "and a little bit ironic, now that I think about it. After the lesson today, I feel like you'll agree with me."

He used the remote in his pocket to click to the next slide. All it said was, "Three is a demon's favorite number."

Rand let that information sink in.

"I thought six was the number of the beast?" The girl—Stacy—sat in the front row every time, always enraptured by the subject material. In all honesty, that alarmed Rand more than it flattered him.

"In the Biblical sense, it is. You'll learn all about that in your other Religious Studies classes. But in my class, we focus on *this* number. It's a more practical approach."

The door at the top of the stadium opened. Rand thought he had a latecomer, but instead, a woman wearing a pantsuit entered and took a seat at the desk closest to the exit. She sat up, straight and stern, and laid a folder of papers in front of her.

"Umm." Rand lost his train of thought.

A few students noticed Rand's distraction and turned to look at the woman. She only crossed her legs, pen poised over her paper, and focused on Rand.

Really? We're going to do this on a Friday? He hadn't seen that particular lady before, but he knew she was yet another auditor sent to scrutinize his class.

"Right," Rand said. "The number three. Why it matters."

He clicked his remote again, and the slide changed to another with pictures.

"I'm sure you are all familiar with the Trinity. The Father, the Son, and the Holy Spirit. The three in one. The Christian God is the one God, but he is also all three beings. Demonic spirits hate God, so they will often use the number three to mock him."

The next slide was a smattering of pictures of clocks. Some digital, some wristwatches, and others antique grandfathers. All of them read three o'clock.

"These are some of my personal photos," Rand explained. "Each was taken in the home of someone I've known or consulted with. Whenever one of these demons was present, their clocks would always stop at three o'clock in the morning."

Rand shot a glance at the woman at the back of his classroom. She stared at the screen now, her note-taking forgotten. She looked confused.

"Why three o'clock in the morning?" Stacy asked, raising her hand, but not waiting to be called on. "Why not three in the afternoon?"

"Great question. It's because demons prefer to operate in darkness. There's still daylight at three o'clock in the afternoon."

Stacy scribbled a note.

"You could have gotten those off Google," said a guy in the third row. Rand knew Garrett. The kid had a C in the class, which was nearly impossible considering he made the course so straightforward. The kid was only enrolled for the easy A and was a skeptic through and through.

"True, Garrett," Rand said. Garrett seemed surprised that Rand remembered his name. "But I didn't."

Rand clicked the remote again. The next slide was of bodies. Lower backs, stomachs, necks, legs. And each of them showed three long, red, and jagged marks gouged into their skin.

"The more violent hauntings usually come with scratches," Rand explained. "Again, these are my own pictures of people I've assisted over the years."

Rand glanced to the back of the class again. The woman used her cell phone to snap a picture of the screen, looking very put off.

Why did she have to choose this lesson? he thought.

Not like many of the others would have been much better.

The group of girls in the center squirmed as they stared at the pictures.

"Could I have also gotten these off Google?" Rand asked Garrett.

Garrett shrugged. "Maybe Photoshop? They are all pretty similar."

"I guess I could have photoshopped them. Except I'm not great at technology. Also…"

Rand untucked his shirt and rolled it up. He turned around and exposed his back to the class. Some students leaned in. "I even have a little souvenir myself."

That had been a painful and violent case. The triple scratch Rand had sustained had scarred. He would carry it for the rest of his life.

As he tucked his shirt back in, the woman in the back seemed appalled.

Maybe I shouldn't be showing skin during an audit. But he always saved his scar for the lesson on the number three.

"Did it hurt?" someone asked.

"Like hell."

"If this kind of stuff happens to you," a girl asked as she

raised her hand, "then why do you… keep doing it? Why don't you stop getting involved?"

"Good question," Rand said. "Until you experience it personally—and I pray you never do—you won't understand how frightening it is. And if you ever do, God forbid, you'll be desperate for someone to help you. That is why I do what I do. And I do it because no one else will."

The class fell silent.

"Now," he said, snapping the attention once again to the lesson at hand. "Three. What other tricky things do these bastards get up to? Let's check it out."

He clicked his remote again. Meanwhile, the woman at the back scribbled on her papers, a frown on her face.

2

His office was a cramped space that Rand was pretty sure had once been used for storage. He walked in and dropped his leather bag on the chair across from his desk, then let himself collapse heavily in the other chair behind his desk.

It was four o'clock in the afternoon and the bright sun shone through the single window. Or it would have if it weren't covered in a white, cloudy smudge. Due to the structure of the old building, the window wasn't easily accessible from the pathway that passed by it. Therefore, the cleaners tended to overlook it.

The office was cluttered with papers and books. The place had become his second home, even though there wasn't enough space to keep up with the things that were accumulating. And there was no way he was in line for a bigger office. Not like the ones the department heads got. His class was the most looked down upon in the whole Religion department. He understood.

There was a knock on the door, and the auditor from

earlier poked her head in. "Good afternoon, Mr. Casey. May I come in?"

Rand stifled a sigh. *So I guess we really* are *going to do this on a Friday.* He supposed it was too much to hope that it could wait until Monday. Without a word, he gestured toward the seat in front of his desk. When the woman found it occupied, Rand quickly removed his bag.

"My name is Doris Galloway," she said, removing the glasses that were resting on the bridge of her nose. "I'm one of the university's head auditors."

"So you're Frank, Susan, and Nelson's boss?" Rand asked, his tone flat. Doris seemed taken aback by that. "They've all visited my class before."

Doris cleared her throat. "Yes, I am their supervisor."

"Got it."

Rand leaned back in his chair. He was no stranger to the auditing process. But this time it seemed they had sent in the big guns to take him down.

People like Doris weren't a problem if you taught freshman algebra or economics. It was the art teachers, music teachers, and paranormal studies instructors who were in constant danger of falling victim to budget cuts.

"I attended your class earlier," Doris explained. She crossed her legs and opened her folder across her thighs. "Very interesting stuff. I took some notes and was hoping to find out more about you."

My official credentials, my teaching experience. Rand had neither and honestly was surprised his class at the university had been allowed to go on as long as it had. He could thank his friend, the Dean, for the job, since he owed Rand a major personal favor. But that had been years ago, and Rand had known it was just a matter of time before the good graces ran their course.

Doris put her glasses back on to keep reading the paperwork. "How long have you been employed at Louisiana State University, Mr. Casey?"

"Rand, please," he said. He folded his hands together and rested them on the desk. "This is my seventeenth semester teaching here. I've found it to be a rewarding experience."

She eyed him over the top of her lenses. "I see. And how many students would you say you have enrolled across all your sections?"

"Four hundred and seventy-eight," he said. "Those are the ones who sign up. Some drop."

"What is your drop rate?" she asked. "Actually, I can look that up to get an accurate—"

"Forty-one percent," Rand said off the top of his head.

"Oh. I see." Doris made a show of clicking her pen and writing the number down in the notes. "I'll still verify it. Why do you think that is? Is your course difficult?"

"No, not at all," Rand said. "It's too frightening."

Doris paused her writing. "I beg your pardon?"

"It's frightening," Rand repeated. "The stuff I teach is real, and it scares the students. Some of them are very interested, and those are the ones I love to have in class. But there are others who can't handle it. I understand."

Doris pursed her lips as she seemed to gather her words. "I don't think I've ever been told that a course is too *frightening*."

"You made it through one lesson," Rand said. "That's better than the students who leave halfway through the first class."

Doris gave a mirthless chuckle. "Perhaps I'm somewhat of a skeptic."

Now she had pushed his button. Dancing around the auditing formalities was one thing, but this was another. "These kids need to know what's out there. Math and economics are part of the real world, sure, but the stuff I teach is just as real, and can be very dangerous for anyone unaware."

Doris stared at him as if he were a crazy person. Good. He was used to that, but he wasn't wrong. The spirits did not discern between age, race, or sex. Doris Galloway, university auditor, was susceptible to their terror, the same as the rest. They did not care if she considered herself a "skeptic."

"I see…" She clicked her pen, but when she brought the tip to the paper, it appeared she could not think of anything to write.

A knock on the door interrupted them.

There stood a young girl, one that Rand recognized from the last section of his class. Stacy Thompson, his front-row fan.

"Hi," she said, hesitating in the hallway. "Am I intruding?"

Doris said, "No, dear. Please, come in. These are Mr. Casey's office hours and *I* am the one who is interrupting. This is your time to speak to your instructor if you need to."

"Oh," the girl said. "Okay. Then…"

Doris vacated her chair and motioned for the girl to sit. She did and moved a piece of blonde hair out of her face and tucked it behind her ear.

"My name is—"

"Stacy Thompson," Rand finished for her. "Section three on Friday afternoons. You currently have an A."

Stacy sat up straight. "Oh. Yeah." She smiled. Even Doris smirked at his memory.

"What can I do for you?" Rand asked.

"I was wondering… for the final exam, is it going to be cumulative?"

The final? They had not even reached midterms yet.

But that was Stacy. He knew the type. Always planning ahead, wanting nothing to threaten her 4.0. He wondered if an A in Paranormal Studies would help someone's transcripts, or just make eyebrows raise.

"Cumulative?" Rand asked.

"Yeah," Stacy said. "Is it going to cover everything we've learned all semester, or is it just the last test? Meaning it only covers material since the test before it."

"Ah, right," Rand said. "Not cumulative. It's just a final test. And it will not be weighted any more than the others."

Doris frowned at that little detail. Other professors in the Religious Studies department always weighted their final exams.

But Rand had always hated weighted and cumulative finals when he was in school. Therefore, in his class— where he was in charge—they were off the table.

"Right. Okay, thank you."

"Is that everything?" Rand asked.

"Yes, Mr. Casey."

She got up and left, casting Doris Galloway a short glance as she went.

Doris resumed her place in the seat across from Rand. "How many students would you say show up to your office hours, Mr. Casey?" she asked, ignoring his request for her to call him by his first name.

"Hmm." Rand wondered if this was a trick question. None of the other auditors had asked him that before. More students coming by could mean they had more questions and concerns about the way he was teaching or grading, which meant more issues. On the other hand, fewer people showing up possibly indicated disinterest. "I have a few trickling in every now and then." Rand shrugged and gave her his best charming smile.

She was unamused. She returned the glasses to her nose and wrote in her papers.

Rand sat across from her in silence for a long time and let her work. He tried to peek at what she was scribbling, but he couldn't read any of her messy scrawl upside down.

Then, Rand noticed another presence outside his office.

One that looked out of a place.

It was a man alongside a woman, presumably husband and wife. They were both middle-aged and most likely not students at the university.

And Rand recognized the looks on their faces—knew them too well. Desperation, terror, and uncertainty.

These people needed his help.

"Good afternoon," Rand said, standing, the audit forgotten. Doris looked up from her work and twisted in her chair to see who had intruded this time.

"Hi," the man said, stepping forward into the office, but only one step. His wife lingered behind him. "We are looking for a Mr. Randolph Casey."

"You've found him," Rand said with a smile. "What can I do you for?"

3

Their nervous demeanor did not change, and Rand felt the smile fade from his face. He saw the urgency in their facial expressions, the tension they held inside.

Doris Galloway, on the other hand, sensed no such thing. "Are you students of Mr. Casey's? Here for his office hours?"

"Oh. No, ma'am," the man said. "But we called ahead and asked when he would be in the office. We were told he would be free during this time."

"He normally is," Doris said, "but if you're not students, then I must ask you to please wait a few minutes. We are having a meeting."

"Oh." He smiled pleasantly, almost masking the pain behind his eyes. "I'm sorry. We'll wait as long as we have to."

"Actually, Doris, I would like to speak with them now." Doris cast him a puzzled look. "Feel free to stay, though."

Doris, not used to being sidelined, eventually rose and

took her place on the far side of the office, where she had stood when Stacy had asked about the midterms.

"Please," Rand said, gesturing to the chair across from his desk. There was only room for one, so the man told his wife to sit, which she did. He stood behind her with a hand on her shoulder.

"My name is Nick Collins." He extended his hand and Rand shook it firmly. "This is my wife, Maria." Rand shook her hand, too.

They were a good-looking couple. Nick was tall and had a firm jaw. His face was barely wrinkled with his age, and the hair on the side of his temples was grey. The rest was brown, and the difference was very stark. Maria looked younger than him, with blonde hair cut short to her shoulders. Her eyes were clear blue, and she wore meticulously applied lipstick on her thin lips. She sat with a straight posture and an air of strength and confidence, but the look of despair on her face ruined her guise. At least to Rand.

"Randolph Casey," Rand said. "But please, call me Rand."

Since Nick was standing, Rand remained standing as well.

Nick's hand brushed the back of his head, rustling his hair. "We uh... we came because..." He and Maria glanced at each other. "We have a problem."

"Sure," Rand said, trying to keep the tone upbeat.

"Well... I don't know how to explain this," Nick said.

"You don't have to worry about sounding silly," Rand said. "Not in this office. Just tell me straight what's going on, and how I can help."

The tension went out of Maria's shoulders, and she

slumped forward. That was a common problem when people came to see him—they thought they were crazy for having the issues they were having.

"We have a daughter," Maria said. "Her name is Georgia. She is hospitalized at St. Mary's Medical Center because she has cystic fibrosis. Are you familiar with the condition?"

"I can't say I am."

"Basically," Nick said, "it causes her body to produce too much mucus in her lungs. There's no cure, and she's spent about a third of her life in the hospital for her surgeries."

"I have a picture," Maria said, diving into her purse. She produced a single photograph, which she handed to Rand, the smile of a proud mother on her face for the first time since she'd come into the office.

One glance told Rand everything. Georgia Collins was a lively and vibrant girl. Even in a photograph, her energy radiated out, her smile reaching her blue eyes completely. An oxygen cannula was in her nostrils and the tubes were tucked behind her ears.

"She's beautiful," Rand said. "How old is she?"

"Fifteen."

That hit Rand in the gut. Only a year younger than his own daughter.

"Looks just like her mother."

Maria's smile widened, but then it dropped as quickly as it came.

"Georgia had a friend," Nick said. "A boy she met at the hospital named Thomas, who was also a CF kid. That's what they call themselves. Anyway, about three months ago, Thomas's health worsened, and he fell into a coma. He died a few days after that."

"Oh," Rand said. "I'm sorry to hear that."

"Yeah. He was a good kid, and only sixteen. They say people with cystic fibrosis can have a life expectancy up to their thirties, but sometimes things happen."

"I understand," Rand said.

In the corner, Doris Galloway focused on the couple, her papers forgotten. Rand even thought he could see tears shimmer in the corners of her eyes.

"Georgia's a little trooper," Maria said. "She's almost always positive and happy, and just an amazing young lady all around. But ever since Thomas passed away, she's been in a funk."

"She lost a friend," Rand said. "Perhaps she's considering the same could happen to her."

"Believe it or not," Nick said, "Georgia talks to us often about dying. She says she isn't afraid, that every day is a blessing, and when her time comes she knows she will have lived her best life."

"That's inspiring," Rand said.

"It is." Nick couldn't help but smile. "So Georgia is not afraid to die."

"She sounds like a remarkable young woman," Rand said. "So… what is it that brings you here today?"

Nick and Maria exchanged a glance. Then Nick spoke. "She told us that Thomas's ghost comes to visit her at night."

Now Rand understood where he fit in.

Doris Galloway's brow furrowed. The sad story had— for her—taken an unusual turn.

"Okay," Rand said.

Nick and Maria seemed surprised at Rand's nonjudgmental answer.

"There are child psychologists and sociologists on staff at the hospital at all times," Maria said. "And we've talked to them a lot about these claims Georgia is making. About talking to and seeing and hanging out with Thomas's ghost at night. The doctors are saying it's her way of grieving. She misses her friend and likes the idea that, even after she passes, she'll still be able to live on."

"Right," Rand said, although his first instinct was always to mistrust the opinion of psychologists and sociologists in scenarios like this. Very smart people, to be sure, but they viewed things too clinically. Too black and white.

Sometimes a more open-minded approach was needed.

"We want our daughter to have the freedom to deal with her situation in any way she needs to," Nick said. "Especially in her condition, where we never know what the next day could bring."

Just like what happened to Thomas, Rand thought.

Maria wiped away the tears that suddenly fell from her eyes. Rand grabbed a nearby box of tissues and offered them to her, which she accepted.

"But usually she's so practical and down to earth," Nick said. "This thing with the ghost, though…"

"Do you believe in life after death, Mr. Collins?" Rand asked.

Nick took a few minutes to ponder it. "You know, I never used to. But since we've almost lost Georgia so many times… I have to say it is a very comforting thought."

"Do you think it's possible for Thomas to have visited Georgia from the other side? Do you believe Georgia when she tells you these things?"

"At first, I wasn't sure," Nick said. He rubbed at his chest as he gathered his words. "But ever since, some odd things have been happening."

"Like what?" Rand asked.

"Tell him about the food," Maria said.

"Yeah," Nick said. "One day, the dietary service workers brought around chicken for lunch. Georgia told us not to eat it because Thomas had warned her not to the night before. Maria and I rarely eat the hospital food anyway, but that evening a lot of the kids in the ward got upset stomachs."

"I see," Rand said. For the first time, a hollow feeling of concern sprouted in his belly.

"And the oxygen tanks," Maria prodded.

"They usually drop off full tanks of O2 for Georgia every morning," Nick said. "But for the past few weeks, every morning we'll wake up and find two of them already at the door before the guys make their rounds."

"And they won't be registered," Maria added. "They're supposed to have a code on them so they can be tracked. Oxygen is considered a drug in the hospital, so they need a tag before they go out. It's like someone took them from storage and brought them straight to Georgia's room. And only hers."

"Georgia thinks it's Thomas trying to look out for her," Nick said. "She says she tells him he can't just bring the tanks—that they have to be tagged first—but he doesn't listen."

"What's weird is that when Thomas was alive," Maria

went on, "he also griped about how long it took the guys to deliver the new oxygen tanks. He said all the registration and tracking was stupid, and that it was only air—no one freaked out about water like they did about oxygen."

"We've seen these things happen with our own eyes," Nick said. "I don't want to sit there and argue with her if this is what she's using to grieve about her friend's passing."

"I understand," Rand said. "What exactly can I help you with?"

"We need to ask someone who has a different point of view," Nick said. "Someone who is a believer. We are surrounded by skeptics and... we just want another opinion to weigh in."

"I can do that," Rand said. "I am most certainly a believer."

"And, from what we hear, an expert," Maria said.

Rand and Doris exchanged a small glance.

"You could say that as well," Rand said.

"We were hoping you could come to the hospital with us one day soon," Nick said. "Meet Georgia. Spend some time and get to know her and ask her about her ghost friend. She doesn't talk about it much anymore, because she knows people don't believe her. If she knew you believed, then she might open up to you."

Rand nodded. "Sounds reasonable."

"Could you also evaluate the situation?" Maria asked. "Can you tell if there really *is* a ghost there?"

"I would be happy to meet Georgia," Rand said to Nick. Then, he turned to Maria. "And I will check for any signs of paranormal activity."

"Thank you," Nick said, very relieved as if he'd considered that Rand might decline. "Thank you so much. That means a lot to my family. We just… need help."

"I understand," Rand said. "I've assisted many people with their supernatural experiences. And your daughter sounds like a lovely girl."

That made Maria smile.

Rand took their phone number and told them he would call to arrange a time to join them at St. Mary's.

As they left, Nick turned and shook his hand. "Thank you again, Mr. Casey."

"Rand, please."

"Rand. Seriously. It's very hard to track down someone who has knowledge about this stuff, and one that doesn't seem kind of… out there."

"I get it," Rand said. Ghosts and spiritualism were definitely fringe topics, and he was happy to bring some professionalism to it.

It was serious business, after all. Even if people like Doris Galloway didn't agree.

The couple left, closing the door behind them. Rand returned to his desk, thoughts of Georgia Collins and her ghostly friend swirling around in his head.

Instinct and experience told him that Georgia *was* communicating with a ghost. A hospital where terminal children frequently passed away? Where parents constantly lived in grief and fear and doubt? The energy in a place like that would easily attract a lost spirit, especially one that was not yet ready to move on.

Doris Galloway cleared her throat and Rand gave her his attention.

"Oh, right. Where were we?"

She removed her glasses. The papers were in her hand,

down by her side. "Is this extracurricular 'investigation' something you do frequently, Mr. Casey?" she asked.

Rand noticed that Maria had forgotten to take back the photograph. Georgia's beaming smile shone up at him from the desk. As if she were not sick at all.

"There's a lot of confusion out there when it comes to this kind of thing, Mrs. Galloway," Rand said. "I always try to be of assistance whenever anyone needs guidance."

"Do you feel this work on the side ever interferes with your focus in the classroom?" Doris asked.

Rand couldn't tear his eyes away from the picture of Georgia. She reminded him of his own daughter.

"Mr. Casey?"

Rand snapped his focus back. "Yes? You were saying?"

Doris only scowled at him. "I think I have all the information I need." She stacked her papers with an air of finality. "Have a good weekend."

4

R and sat at his kitchen table with his laptop open. He wore only boxer shorts and a white undershirt. He had seven tabs open at the top of the screen, each one about Georgia's condition.

Cystic fibrosis.

He scrolled through the articles, becoming more and more depressed at each one he read.

How is it fair for a child to get such a sickness?

And then, on top of it all, to be visited by a ghost. Georgia's picture rested on the table beside his computer. Every time he glanced at it, he couldn't help but smile himself.

He was so lost in his thoughts that a sudden movement startled him.

Rachel set down a cup of hot tea. "Whoa. A little bit jumpy, are we?" She wore only his shirt, her long legs bare underneath the hem.

"Where did you learn to sneak like that?" he said. "And thank you."

She leaned over his shoulder and looked at the monitor. "Studying for medical school?"

"I wish."

Rand closed the laptop and stood. He took her in his arms and looked down into her green eyes.

"You've been quiet this evening," Rachel said. "Everything all right?"

"Yeah. Just a crazy day at work."

She smiled. "How crazy can it be being a college professor?"

He smirked. "You have no idea."

There was an aggressive knock on the door, and then it opened.

"Dad!"

It was only then that Rand realized he'd forgotten about Libby.

"Dad!" Libby, his sixteen-year-old daughter, came around the corner of the living room and into the kitchen. She stopped short when she saw Rand and Rachel just pulling out of their embrace.

Libby gave Rachel a quick smile. "Hey, Rachel." Then she glared at Rand. "I thought we were meeting up tonight, Dad."

Blonde-haired and tall for her age, Libby reminded Rand of Georgia Collins. Or maybe the girl had just been on his mind all afternoon.

Rand brought his hand to his forehead. "Libby, I'm sorry. It totally slipped my mind. It's just that work… "

Then Tessa appeared behind Libby. He felt Rachel tense up beside him.

Oh, great, Rand thought. Rachel hadn't yet met Libby's mother, and if it were up to him, it wouldn't have happened until their relationship was much further along.

"So everyone's here," Rand muttered under his breath. "Just what I need…" He rolled his eyes.

Tessa looked Rachel up and down, making no effort to hide it. "I see you have company. Maybe we should come back some other time."

"No," Libby said. "We can't come back. We have to get this figured out now."

"Phones are a thing, you know," Rand told Tessa. "You could've called and let me know you were planning to grace me with your presence tonight."

"We *tried* calling, Rand," Tessa said, putting her hands on her hips.

Rand remembered he was standing there in his underwear. His phone must've still been in his pants pocket in the bedroom.

"I'm Rachel," Rachel said timidly to Tessa, stepping forward and extending her hand. Tessa took it with a limp wrist.

"This is Tessa, Libby's mother," Rand said.

"Nice to meet you. Excuse me," Rachel said, then slipped back into the bedroom.

"Pretty girl," Tessa said coldly. Then to Libby, "I see you've met her?"

"Yeah," Libby said. "I come over here all the time."

"You didn't tell me he was seeing someone new."

"You wanted to know?"

Tessa didn't answer.

"Libby, I'm sorry," Rand said, trying to get the conversation back on topic. "I completely forgot you were coming over tonight. Something crazy happened at work today."

"How crazy can a teaching job be?" Libby crossed her arms. "But you remembered that we're going hiking tomorrow, right?"

That had slipped his mind as well. "Oh."

Libby visibly deflated. "Dad. Come on, you promised. You said you wouldn't cancel!"

"Yeah, I know," Rand said, running a hand through his hair. "But something came up."

Rachel came back into the kitchen. She was wearing her jeans and t-shirt again and had brought Rand his own pants. Rand took them but didn't put them on.

"Something came up?" Libby asked. "What do you mean?" She glanced at Rachel. "You two are hanging out tonight, so can't I have my dad tomorrow for the hiking trip he's been promising to take me on forever?"

Rachel's eyes went wide. "Wait, what? Rand and I don't have plans tomorrow."

"Rachel isn't what suddenly came up," Rand told his daughter.

Libby looked back at him. "Then what?"

"Umm." Rand felt all the eyes on him.

"Randolph," Tessa said, folding her arms. "You've been putting this hike off for a long time. What could possibly be so important?"

"It's something that happened at work," he said. "I'd rather not say."

Libby gave him a look. "You only have one class on Fridays."

"I know. Come and sit." He led the way into the living

room and everyone followed him. Tessa and Libby sat on the couch while Rachel continued to stand, arms folded across her chest. Rand had not intended for her to meet his ex that night—or ever, if he'd had his way. But hey, these things happen. He could get it all back on track. No problem.

Libby looked up at him expectantly.

"So, I was in the office today, and I was visited by a couple. They told me about their daughter."

Rand told them the whole story. As he did, he became very aware of Rachel's growing confusion. Libby and Tessa, however, looked bored.

Libby already knew where this was going.

"This is different," Rand told his daughter. "Her parents are emotional right now. I need to go in there and help them set things straight. Understand?"

Libby sighed. "Do you have to go tomorrow?"

"Libby, think of this family and their situation."

"All right," Libby said, without considering for long. She stood and hugged her dad. Rand embraced her back. "I knew you were going to cancel on me because of a case. You haven't had one coming in a while, and I knew you were due for one."

Rand kissed his daughter on the top of her head. "I know. This will be a quick one. In and out, send the spirit on its way. Then we can hike on Sunday."

"I told Bailey I'd hang out with her on Sunday," Libby said.

"Invite her along."

Libby shrugged. "I don't think she'd be into it, but sure."

"So," Rachel said, speaking for the first time in a while.

She eyed Rand. "I thought you were a religious studies professor."

Libby rounded on her father. "You haven't told her?"

Tessa smirked and leaned back on the couch, ready to watch it all unfold.

Rand rubbed the back of his head again. "Umm."

"Told me what?" Rachel asked.

"I *am* a religious studies professor," Rand said. "I mean… my class is listed under the Religious Studies department. My actual class, though… is about paranormal activity."

The room was silent for a very long time.

"You mean like… ghosts?"

"Yeah."

Her brow furrowed as if her brain was trying to figure out if it had processed that correctly. "You teach a class about ghosts?"

"Well. Yeah. But not just about ghosts. About the spiritual side of death, resurrection, the afterlife, and how ghosts sometimes get trapped here on earth. And how we can recognize them, and how to deal with them when we encounter them."

"Oh," Rachel said, although Rand could tell he was losing her. "And… people come to you as some sort of expert on this?"

"It's been known to happen."

"You called this a 'case.' Lawyers have cases."

"Right," Rand said. "So yeah, I guess it happens a decent bit."

"And so you're, like, a teacher by day, ghost hunter by night?"

"Well…" Rand searched for the words. "Paranormal

activity mostly happens at night. It's the best time to detect them."

"Show her your room of equipment," Tessa said, the smirk still on her face.

Rand shushed her.

"Equipment?" Rachel asked.

In truth, Rand was not embarrassed or ashamed of what he did at all. Quite the contrary. But when it came to his romantic relationships—particularly the new ones— he had to be careful about how he revealed the details. Most of them were skeptics, and their acceptance was usually easier after they had been dating for a while. But he and Rachel had only been seeing each other for just over three weeks.

"I think I should go," Rachel said.

Without waiting, she took her keys from the table and walked toward the door.

"Rachel, wait," Rand began, but without another word, she was gone.

I'll definitely have to do some damage control later, Rand thought.

"I can't believe you hadn't told her," Libby said.

"It's only been three weeks!" Rand retorted. "You shouldn't have brought it up!"

"*You* brought it up," Libby shot back.

"Only because you demanded I tell you why I couldn't take you hiking!"

"I have a right to know why you're canceling on me again! And why don't you put your pants on?"

Rand snatched his pants from the coffee table and shoved his legs into them. He hopped up and down as he yanked them on, almost tumbling over. "The most important thing here is the Collins family. I'm going to meet them tomorrow at St. Mary's."

Libby sighed. "Okay. I'll get over it. Sorry for messing up your evening with Rachel."

"How old is she, by the way?" Tessa asked from the couch.

"Mom!" Libby said.

"Here, take a look at this picture," Rand said, ignoring Tessa and walking to the kitchen. He returned with the photograph of Georgia. "She's your age, you know."

Libby studied the picture for a long time, then broke out into a smile. "She seems so happy."

"I know. That's why it's so crazy that she's sick."

"What does she have?"

"Cystic fibrosis. Ever heard of it?"

"Yeah, but I don't know what it does to you. I'll google it." Libby looked up. "I want to meet her."

"What? Why?"

"Because she seems nice. Take me with you tomorrow."

"I don't know if that's such a good idea. They're only expecting me."

"Come on, Dad. Please?"

"Maybe some other time." He took the picture from Libby and dropped it on the coffee table as if doing that would make her forget her request. Libby could be quite stubborn, and once she got an idea in her head she rarely let it drop.

LATER THAT NIGHT, just before he went to bed, his phone rang. It was Rachel.

"Hey," she said sleepily.

"Hey. You all right?"

"Yeah," she said.

"Sorry about earlier. I forgot Libby was supposed to come over. She usually doesn't bring her mother, though."

"It's no problem. Tessa's very pretty."

Rand ignored that. "And I'm sorry for not mentioning the other thing. It's true—I'm a ghost hunter on the side, for lack of a better term. I still spend most of my time teaching, though." He let the words hang there, but Rachel said nothing, waiting for him to elaborate. "It's just every now and then, the material I teach... word kind of gets around. People start realizing that they've experienced these things before and they get curious, or afraid. So they come to me and tell me they're scared and don't know what to do. Most people don't believe them when they say they are dealing with a haunting. So I feel obligated to step in and help them out."

"I know," Rachel said. "I get it. I've thought about it a lot, and it all sounds kind of crazy to me, but I can get around it. I can find a way."

Rand rolled over in bed, slightly confused. This was usually when women broke up with him. "You're all right with it?"

"Yeah. I mean, you're helping people, right?"

"They tell me I helped them."

"And not hurting anyone?"

"No, of course not."

"And not scamming anyone?"

"Please. I never take money for these types of cases."

"Okay. Then I would love to hear more about it."

"Good. Maybe you can come hiking with me and Libby on Sunday?"

"I think you should spend that time with your daughter. The next night we can go for dinner and you can tell me all about what you found at St. Mary's. I feel so bad for that girl."

"Me too," Rand said. "I'll call you tomorrow, okay?"

"Good night, Rand."

He set the phone down and rolled over again. As he drifted off, he reconsidered the conversation. Perhaps it would've been best if they had broken up.

Although the relationship was new and showed a lot of promise, Rand knew from experience that his investigations and his relationships rarely mixed well. When he got involved with a case, the supernatural tended to affect him along with his client, which meant his past girlfriends had experienced terrifying situations that they didn't deserve. The last thing he wanted was for that trend to continue with Rachel.

This case should be straightforward enough, Rand told himself. *If there's a ghost, send it away, and everyone moves on. In and out. Simple and easy.*

5

S t. Mary's was the largest hospital in the city, but Rand had never fully realized just how huge it was. It was the first time he had ever been there, and it was like its own miniature town rather than a medical facility.

Weaving his way into the parking garage, he would have gotten lost had it not been for the clear signs, the bright arrows painted on the asphalt, and the occasional worker wearing a yellow vest, waving him in.

Going above and beyond, he thought, impressed with the ease of finding a spot when the garage was already so full.

The lobby reminded him of the atrium entrance of a large mall rather than a hospital. His footsteps echoed off the high walls, and many hallways branched off that main section. The reception desk in front of him seemed like a logical place to start.

Rand approached a friendly woman, who greeted him with a smile. It was genuine—Rand got good vibes from the woman. "Good afternoon, sir. Welcome to St. Mary's."

"Hi there," Rand said. "I was wondering if you could point me to the coffee shop."

"Certainly. Which one?"

Rand chuckled. He should have figured there'd be more than one in a place this size. "Your nearest."

"The Bean Factory is our own personal brand. We import the finest coffees from all over the world." She pointed toward a corridor that led away from the main lobby. "If you go this way and turn right, it will be on your left."

Rand smirked. Her sales pitch was well-practiced. "Thank you very much."

"You're welcome. Have a blessed day."

Rand followed the woman's directions, looking around as he did. Hospitals usually gave him the creeps, but at St. Mary's he didn't even feel like he was in a hospital. A man in a suit passed him going the other way, an employee badge dangling from his coat. He nodded at Rand when he saw him and wished him a good afternoon.

The coffee shop was exactly where the greeter said it would be. Nick and Maria Collins sat in the corner, talking low between themselves.

When Maria noticed him, she gave him a small smile and stood. Nick followed her gaze, spotted him, and did the same.

"Thank you for coming," Nick said, shaking his hand. "You made it here alright? We figured this would be the easiest place to meet in this huge place."

"No problem at all," Rand said. "Should we get started?"

"You want to grab something before we go?" Nick

pointed his thumb toward the counter, where a young girl enthusiastically took orders.

"Had my coffee in the car," Rand said.

Nick looked away as he slowly nodded. Rand saw that he was nervous.

"We can head up, then," Nick said.

"Perfect. You lead the way."

NICK AND MARIA brought him deeper into St. Mary's to an elevator, which they rode to the tenth floor.

The doors opened to the entrance of the ward. A single security guard manned the desk, and he smiled and rose when he saw Nick and Maria.

"We're back," Maria said.

"Sure thing." The man nodded and handed them a clipboard where they could sign in.

"This is a friend," Nick said, nodding his head toward Rand. "Wanted to introduce him to Georgia."

Rand extended his hand, and the security guard took it. "Randolph Casey."

"Harold," said the guard. "I'm the main security on duty up here." He was a stout black man, with a round frame filling out his beige uniform. What hair remained on his head was short and grey.

"Pleased to meet you."

"Meeting Georgia for the first time, hmm? Good luck in there, my friend."

"Will I need it?"

"That girl's one of a kind." He couldn't help but smile as he said it.

"So I hear."

Harold took the clipboard away and replaced it with a binder, which he opened. "Simple process for non-relative visitors. Sign in here, then we'll give you a name tag. When you leave, you'll sign out."

"No problem," Rand said. He produced his own pen from his pocket and signed his name. Harold gave him a name tag sticker, with "RANDOLPH" already written in big black letters.

Rand put it on his chest. "Next time, just Rand. It's what friends call me."

Harold nodded and smiled. "No problem, Mr. Rand."

Rand thought he saw a knowing look in the security guard's eyes, and he wondered if someone had told him who he was and what he was there to do.

WHEN RAND FOLLOWED Nick and Maria into room 1019, it was like he'd stepped out of a hospital and into the bedroom of a teenage girl. There were posters of singers on her walls, and around them were photographs of her and her friends. There was a desk in the corner stacked with schoolwork and a vase of flowers. Someone had recently burned a floral-scented candle. The hospital bed had been removed and replaced with a single, narrow bed, with a fluffy pink comforter and a bunch of pillows.

Georgia propped herself against the headboard, a computer on her lap, knees bent up. An oxygen tube ran from her nostrils to a fixture on the wall.

"We're back," Maria said.

Georgia closed her laptop. She and Rand met eyes, and

she gave him a beaming smile, the same as in the photograph he had. "Is this the ghost man?"

Rand couldn't help but laugh. "Yes, I am the ghost man. Randolph Casey. Friends call me Rand." He offered his hand and Georgia took it, giving it a single, dramatic pump.

"Georgia Collins. Friends call me Georgia. Nice to meet you, Rand."

"I guess that means we're friends."

She threw her legs over the edge of the bed and sat up. She wore an oversized t-shirt, black leggings, and socks, one that was blue and the other orange. Her blonde hair was wavy.

"You knew he was coming," Maria told her daughter. "You couldn't have put something else on?"

"Take me as I am," Georgia told Rand, spreading her arms.

"Will do." Already Rand felt her warmth and vibrancy.

"Have a seat," Nick said, pulling up a chair from the other side of the room.

"This is exciting," Georgia said, eyeing Rand. "A real-life ghost man."

"I take it you've never met a ghost man before," Rand said.

"All I ever get to meet are doctors, nurses, and psychologists. This is so cool. I hope you know I'm going to tell all my friends about you."

Rand laughed. "Fine by me."

"Come on," Georgia said. "I'll give you a tour of the place."

Maria sat up straight. "Honey, Mr. Rand just got here. I'm sure he doesn't want to walk around the whole place."

"It's fine," Rand said, standing. "I actually would appreciate a tour. I've never been inside St. Mary's before."

That, and Rand already knew he wanted to separate Georgia from her parents if he was going to ask her about the ghost she was seeing. He figured it was the best way to get her to open up fully about her experience.

Georgia unhooked her tubing from the device on the wall, which hissed before she twisted the knob to turn off the oxygen. She hooked up to a portable tank on wheels, which was inside a black bag that looked like a rolling suitcase. Then she donned a pair of oversized and ridiculous purple sunglasses, and said, "Shall we?"

6

"This is the tenth ward—for children, so that's why it's got all these kiddie things on the wall," Georgia explained as they strolled. "I'm under eighteen, so they still put me here instead of a normal ward. I'm, like, the oldest person here, I think. Or I am now that Thomas died. Did my parents tell you about Thomas?"

"They mentioned him, yes," Rand said.

"Yeah. He was another CF kid and, like, my best friend for a while. He lived here too, but we only really talked on video chat."

"Why is that?" Rand asked.

They passed by the nurses' station and Georgia waved her hand like she was a pageant queen. "Hello, hello, everyone." The three nurses behind the desk all stopped what they were doing to tell her good afternoon.

Georgia said, "I'm definitely the favorite around here."

"I can see that," Rand said. "So why did you and Thomas only talk on video chat?"

"Oh yeah. It's a CF thing. People with CF shouldn't be around other people with CF. Don't tell anyone, but we totally used to meet up sometimes, anyway. But we'd wear masks, so it's cool, right? Hospital masks, not like Halloween masks. Although that would've been fun."

"Your secret is safe with me," Rand said.

Harold the security guard sat at his desk near the elevator.

"Miss Georgia," he said when he saw her coming. "Loving those stunner shades."

"I wish I'd known, I would have gotten you a pair." Georgia and Harold high-fived each other over the desk. "I'm heading down for some ice cream with my new boyfriend. Call me on the secret phone if you need help taking down any perps."

"Will do, Miss Georgia."

She pressed the down button on the elevator.

As they waited, Rand said, "You're going to start rumors around here about us."

"Be proud, Ghost Man. I'm quite a catch."

The elevator dinged, and they got inside.

"By the way, I'm on antibiotics right now and it kind of makes me sensitive to bright light. That's why I'm wearing sunglasses. I mean, I'm a freak, but at least I know it's not normal to wear sunglasses inside."

"Doesn't bother me," Rand said. "The sun never sets on being a badass."

Georgia looked up at him for a few seconds. "You're right. I think I'm going to like you."

The elevator opened on the ground floor and Georgia led him down the giant corridor. "The cafeteria here is pretty good. I've had everything on the menu like three times. We're gonna get ice cream, by the way. The ice cream there is totally awesome. It's soft serve. Hey, Mr. Steve." Georgia held out her hand and high-fived a guy in a suit as he passed.

"Looking good, Georgia," he said.

"Have a good day administrating."

"I will."

Georgia said, "That's Steve, one of the hospital administrators. Like, big boss. He asks me before he fires people, though."

"You should tell him I found his parking garage to be easy to navigate."

"I will!" Georgia lit up. "Seriously, that would make him so happy to hear."

The St. Mary's cafeteria was the size of a large restaurant and a myriad of sweet and spicy aromas filled the air. The walls of the dining area were all floor-to-ceiling windows, which looked out over a garden. Some of the employees had taken their lunch outside to enjoy the autumn weather.

"I don't get why they do this," Georgia said, pointing to a podium at the entrance of the cafeteria. There was a plate with the day's main dish—salmon with a red sauce, covered in a clear plastic container. The food already looked like it had grown cold and gross. "I mean, I know they're trying to show it off, but look at it! It doesn't take long for it to start rotting."

"I agree," Rand said.

Georgia led him to the soft-serve ice cream machine. "Chocolate, vanilla, or strawberry?" she asked.

"All three," Rand told her.

"I knew it! We're spirit animals." She grabbed a cup and pulled on the levers one by one.

"Soul mates?"

"Right. What did I say?" She handed the cup to him and then prepared her own ice cream. They walked to the cash registers, where an elderly woman with glasses was ringing people up. "Oh, sweet! Mrs. Eloise is working. Check this out." She elbowed him in the ribs.

"Good afternoon, Miss Georgia," said Mrs. Eloise. "Ice cream for lunch?"

"They brought lunch up to the room today." She turned and winked at Rand when Mrs. Eloise wasn't looking.

"And who is this?" she asked, eyeing Rand up and down.

"My new boyfriend. It's our first date."

"What have I told you about older men, Miss Georgia?"

"I know, but I have to make these mistakes for myself. Duh!"

Mrs. Eloise smiled and pressed a button on her computer, which made the cash drawer open, but she only pushed it closed again. "It's on me."

"Thank you!"

Georgia grabbed the sleeve of Rand's jacket and pulled him away as if trying to move him along before Mrs. Eloise changed her mind.

She took two plastic spoons from the counter on the other side of the register and they sat at a table in the far corner of the dining area.

"Mmm," Georgia said after her first bite of ice cream.

"See? It's the best. Even better than those expensive places they have downtown."

Rand tasted the ice cream, and he had to admit it was actually pretty damn good.

"So, like, how much are my parents paying you to come here and talk to me?" Georgia asked.

"They're not paying me anything."

"Really? Wow. You could totally charge top dollar for being the best ghost man in town."

"I'm the only ghost man in town."

"Then you can charge even more. It's like a *neech*."

"A *niche*."

"So, basically, everyone thinks I'm crazy because I see Thomas around. But doesn't it make sense that I would see him?"

"It does, believe it or not," Rand said. "Spirits who linger in our world feel they weren't ready to pass away when they did. Maybe it was too soon, or it was tragic, or they felt like they had unfinished business."

Georgia's mouth fell open as she stared at him. "Wow. Thomas fits all three of those." She took another bite of ice cream. "It's also so cool to talk to someone who believes in this stuff. Everyone else tries to make me think 'rationally.' "

"I'm definitely a believer," Rand said. "It's very real. Do you believe in life after death?"

Georgia shrugged. "I guess I do now. I mean, sometimes I visit the chapel here and Father Calvin talks about God and Jesus and how we go to heaven when we die. Not sure if I only like the idea of it because I'm so close to dying or because it actually makes sense. You know?"

"Close to dying?" Rand asked.

"Yeah. CF people don't live very long. And about a month ago I collapsed and had to go to the emergency room and all this stuff. My parents don't even like it when I walk around—they say I should use a wheelchair because my lungs are so shitty, but I don't like that. The only reason they let me go now is because you're here and they didn't want to get into a fight about it in front of you. So basically I'm using you for free ice cream and to walk on my own two legs like a normal person." She chuckled. "But seriously. They've given me a year, or maybe two. The doctors say I need a lung transplant."

Rand frowned.

"I'm over it," Georgia said. "I've known my life would be short all along and don't have any regrets. I feel like I'm making the most of every day."

"That's good."

"Do you think that's why I can see Thomas?" Georgia said. "Because I'm so close to the end? I read something like that on the internet."

Rand cleared his throat and put his empty ice cream cup on the table. "Sometimes people are more in tune with the spiritual world when they are closer to joining it themselves."

"Wow," Georgia said. "Since you're the ghost man, do you think we'd be able to hang out after—"

"I would like to think you would move on. As you said, you don't have any regrets and live every day to the fullest. What reason would you have to stay behind?"

"To haunt people," Georgia said, dropping her spoon into her empty cup. "Rattle chains and all that stuff."

Rand smiled and shook his head.

"Why are you laughing at me?" Georgia asked.

"I'm not. It's just that you remind me of my daughter."

"Your daughter must be awesome."

"She is. She's sixteen."

"Really? I want to meet her."

"She said the same thing about you."

"No way!"

"Yes way."

"That settles it. You gotta give me her number." Georgia reached into her pocket and pulled out her cell phone. She unlocked it and passed it across the table to him. The screen was cracked so badly that it looked like it had been shot. Rand didn't move. "What's wrong? Don't mix business and personal stuff or whatever?"

Finally, Rand tapped the phone app on her screen and added Libby's number to her contacts. "Her name is Libby. She texts all the time, so I'm sure you'll get a response if you send her a message."

"Sweet," Georgia said, taking her phone back. "Making new friends is awesome. Makes me feel more normal."

"So now that I've made you a friend," Rand said, "why don't you tell me a little more about Thomas?"

"Ah. Nothing for free from this guy, I see."

"Not like that. I'm just interested in your experience."

"Do you want to know about alive Thomas or dead Thomas?"

"Both."

"Hmm." She rolled her eyes up to the ceiling as she recollected. "Well, alive Thomas was cool. He was sixteen, and he stayed on a different floor than me, and the nurses wouldn't let us hang out, but I told you that already. Hmm, what else? He liked rock-and-roll music and college football. He said he always wanted to play, but his lungs were shit. He had a crush on some girl named Kristen, who volunteers on his floor, but she avoided him when he asked her out because I guess she doesn't like sick boys. Ugh." She stuck out her tongue. "Anyway, he deserves much better. Or, he deserved, I guess. He crashed about three months ago. Health just went splat. Went into a coma, they had to operate, but then he never woke up. I cried at his funeral."

"He sounds like a pretty normal teenager," Rand said. "Sorry for your loss."

"Yeah." She sat in her chair with her hands between her thighs, staring off to the side through her dark sunglasses. For the first time, her energy seemed to leave her as she reminisced about her friend. "It really messed me up when he died," she said after a few seconds. "Even though I've totally been at peace with the whole dying young thing… I don't know. I guess when he passed it made my situation all more real."

"I can't imagine it was easy," Rand said.

"But then he came back. Started visiting me in my room as a ghost."

Rand leaned forward and folded his hands together on the table. "When does he visit you?"

"At night. Like, really late at night. Or early in the morning, whatever you want to call it. He wakes me up every time, which is kind of annoying, but then again he's a ghost, so what does he care?"

"Does he speak to you?"

"Not really," Georgia said. "He's mostly just *there*. Watching. It would be creepy if it wasn't Thomas. I try to talk to him, and it looks like he wants to answer, but I can't hear anything. His mouth never moves."

"What do you say to him?"

"Nothing much. Just ask him what he's doing or if he's okay. Once, I asked if it hurts being dead. I also tell him not to watch me shower and call him a pervert."

"I see. What is he wearing when you see him?"

"The hospital gown." Georgia wrinkled her nose. "Which is weird, because Thomas hated wearing those, and never did."

Rand also found that strange. Usually ghosts appeared as they had when they were alive.

"And how do you feel when Thomas is present?"

Georgia looked at him and removed her sunglasses for the first time. "I don't know. Curious? I mean, there's a ghost standing in my room, so I, like, want to know everything about what it's like to be dead. But he won't tell me anything. Which, now that I think about it, is totally a Thomas thing to do. He could be such a punk sometimes." She smiled.

"Does it bring you comfort to have someone watch over you?"

"Yeah. But if he was my guardian angel, then I figured he would be more intentional about it. He just stands there and stares. Shouldn't you be writing all this down?"

Rand tapped his temple. "It's all up here."

"You don't think I'm crazy, do you? Everyone else thinks I'm nuts."

"Not at all," Rand said. "Encountering the spiritual

world is a lot more common than you realize. It's a special gift you should be proud of."

That made her smile, although Rand had not been completely honest. Usually it was more of a dangerous liability, as it was in his case.

Georgia opened a flap on her black bag and checked her oxygen tank. "I'm low."

7

When they returned to the room, Nick and Maria were sitting on Georgia's bed, watching the news on television. They stood when Rand and Georgia walked in.

"Hey, now. I know these doors don't lock from the inside, but you should at least hang something on the handle," Georgia said.

"Come on, honey," Maria said. "Not in front of guests."

Georgia unhooked her cannula from the portable oxygen cylinder and reattached it to the wall fixture. She twisted the knob to get it flowing again.

"How was the tour?" Nick asked Rand.

"She's a fantastic guide."

"You can leave a tip," Georgia said.

"It was great to meet you today, Georgia," Rand said.

"Aw, leaving already? I thought we would watch TV. Or talk about ghosts some more."

"I'll come back," Rand said. When he said that, Nick and Maria gave him a worried look.

"Are you sure I'm not crazy?" Georgia asked. "Do I have sanity problems on top of my lung problems?"

Rand laughed. "Of course you're not crazy."

"Tell *them* that, please," Georgia said, nodding toward her parents.

"We don't think you're crazy," Maria said. "It's just... we're curious."

"Right," Georgia said, smirking. "Is this the part where y'all go out in the hall and talk about me?"

"I actually think that's a good idea," Rand said.

Nick and Maria followed Rand out into the hallway. Before the door closed, Georgia shouted after him, "Tell them I haven't lost my mind!"

Nick and Maria stood close to Rand in a small huddle, Maria with her arms folded across her chest and Nick with his hands in his pockets. They wore worried expressions as if Rand was a doctor about to give them bad news.

"Your daughter is quite the character," Rand said. His attempt to ease their tension worked, and they chuckled.

"Hope she wasn't too much," Nick said.

"Not at all. She has an amazing outlook, considering her situation."

"She's always been that way, thank the Lord," Maria said. "No matter what comes, she'll always find a way to smile."

"She seems truly special," said Rand. "And I want to help."

"Do you think she needs help? With this... little problem."

"First, we need to determine if it's a problem at all," Rand told them.

"Okay. And how do we go about doing that?"

"Georgia said that when the spirit visits her, she speaks with him and gets the impression he's trying to respond, but she can't hear anything. He is most likely responding, but she's unable to discern it because of the divide between the realms in which they're existing." Nick and Maria gave him a blank stare. "I know it sounds far out there, but trust me. I've been doing this a while."

"So what do you propose?" Nick asked. For the first time, he looked frightened.

"In my bag, I have an EVP recorder. That stands for electronic voice phenomenon. It's the practice of using a device to pick up voices from the spiritual world. I hope to capture their conversation so I can know what the spirit is saying to her. From there, we'll make the judgment call if its presence is helping Georgia cope with her situation, or if it's harmful."

Nick let out a long breath. "I have to say, this stuff is really weird to me. I almost can't believe I'm having this discussion right now. But with all we've been through with Georgia, I guess nothing should surprise me anymore." Maria put a hand on her husband's arm.

"I know what you mean," Rand said. "And I understand. But your mind is open to the possibility, and that's good."

Nick nodded.

"And another thing. I want to plant the recorder without Georgia's knowledge. If she knows it's there, it could alter the natural results."

"Okay," Nick said.

"I'll come back tomorrow and check the recorder. If Georgia says Thomas didn't appear, then I'll change out the batteries and we'll try again. I'll keep coming as long as I have to until we get a positive recording."

At that, Maria's eyes widened. "I didn't realize this would be such a process."

"With the paranormal, we have to be flexible," Rand said with a shrug.

"And uh…" Nick scratched at the stubble on his beard. "How much do we owe you for your services?"

"Nothing," Rand said.

"What?"

"I don't charge for what I do. I am happy to help."

Nick leaned back and let out the large breath he'd been holding. "It's just, with the hospital bills and the procedures—"

Rand held up a hand to stop him. "I understand. The last thing people need when dealing with the paranormal is having to worry about how they will pay."

"Again, thank you so much," Maria said.

"My pleasure."

They went back inside, where Georgia had resumed looking at her computer and leaning against the many pillows on her headboard. "I hope you said good things about me."

"Of course," Rand said.

"I shot your daughter a text, by the way."

"She'll be excited to hear from you."

Maria said, "Rand, would you like some of this cake? One of Georgia's friends brought it by yesterday, but it's so big we couldn't finish."

"No, thank you. Still full from the ice cream."

"And there's plenty more where that came from,"

Georgia said, sitting up. "As long as Mrs. Eloise is working, that is. I have to pee."

"Georgia!" Maria chided.

She removed her cannula and shuffled to the bathroom.

As soon as the door closed, Rand reached into his satchel, which he'd left on the floor near the room's entrance, and pulled out the small recorder. He pressed the button on the side and double-checked that the battery was full. Then he hit the record button and placed it under Georgia's bed.

Nick and Maria watched him as he worked.

The toilet flushed. As she walked out, Georgia waved her hand under an antiseptic dispenser on the wall and it squirted some into her palm.

"I have to hit the road," Rand told her. "It was a pleasure to meet you."

"You too, Ghost Man. When are you coming back?"

"Maybe tomorrow. Or the day after."

"Wow. I must need lots of evaluation."

"I'm only in it for the ice cream."

Georgia laughed. She plopped down onto her bed and placed the cannula into her nostrils. "I'll see you then."

Rand couldn't help but smile. Georgia definitely reminded him of his own daughter. He quickly glanced toward the bottom of her bed where the recorder was hidden. The last thing this girl needed was to be bothered by a spirit who no longer belonged in the world of the living.

He found himself hoping, maybe even praying, that his findings would be benign.

8

Although it was an early fall morning, Rand felt no chill. The sun was bright and clear, warming him, and he reveled in the fresh air.

He reached the top of the rock hill he'd been chugging away at, a small amount of sweat soaking his grey t-shirt.

Forty years old and I've still got it. The hiking, along with a consistent gym routine, kept his body more muscular than most men his age. That and his thick black hair consistently made people think he was younger than he actually was.

When he turned, Libby was only halfway up, face buried in her phone. Her friend Bailey struggled, wavering side to side with each step, hands on her hips as if she had cramps.

"What's going on?" Rand shouted down at them. "We're making terrible time."

Libby looked up and shielded her eyes from the sun with her hand. "What's the rush?"

"This needs to at least somewhat resemble exercise."

"Being on the volleyball team at school isn't enough?" Libby asked, resuming her texting. "I don't need to do anything extra."

Rand sat on a rock and tightened the laces on his hiking boots while he waited for the girls to join him. Libby reached the top of the hill first, and Bailey struggled up a few minutes later.

"Y'all go on," she said, panting and face beet-red. "Leave me here to die."

"It's not that bad," Rand said. "Can you tell my daughter to get off her phone?"

"Libby, your dad says get off your phone."

Libby ignored them both.

"Who is she texting?"

"Probably Justin."

"Who the hell is Justin?"

Libby shot her friend a look. "Bailey!"

"You didn't tell him?"

"Who is Justin?" Rand asked again.

"He's no one," Libby insisted.

"He's her *boyfriend*," Bailey said.

"Not a boyfriend," Libby said. "We're just talking."

"Looks like texting," Rand said. "Show me a picture of him."

"What? No. Don't be weird."

"Come on, I want to see this guy."

"Why?"

"Because I can tell everything I need to know just by looking at him."

"You don't need to know anything about him." Libby

turned her back, thumbs working furiously on the screen. Something in her texts made her smile.

Rand turned to Bailey. "Bailey." He waved her over.

"Yeah, I've got him on Instagram."

"Bailey!" Libby cried.

Bailey took out her phone, brought up Justin's Instagram, and showed Rand. All he saw was a skinny kid with black hair that was too long, a bunch of pimples, weird glasses, and a guitar.

"He looks like a dweeb," Rand said.

"He is not!" Libby said. "And no one says dweeb anymore."

"Then why did I just say it?"

"Because you're being rude. You've never even met him."

"He really is nice, Mr. Rand," Bailey said.

"Does he play football? Or do MMA?"

"No. Guitar."

"Let me hear some of his songs." Rand stood and led the way down the other side of the hill.

"I don't think he has any."

"Why does he bother playing guitar if he doesn't record any music? What good is that?"

"Dad!" Libby shouted again.

The hill's slope increased and Rand turned his body sideways to get better traction with his boots. He let momentum take him and jogged the rest of the way down the hill. "Lot of rocks down here, so don't stare at the phone," Rand called back to the girls.

"Here's a good way to change the subject," Libby said when she fell in beside her father. "You'll never guess who just texted me. Georgia Collins."

"Who is that?" Bailey asked.

"Yeah, she told me she did," Rand said. "She's a nice girl. Reminds me a lot of you. I think you two would get along."

"She invited me to hang out with her at St. Mary's," Libby said. "That was quick."

"She's really friendly. You should go up to visit her sometime."

"I asked you to take me when you went, but you refused."

"Now that I've met her and assessed the situation, you can go," Rand said.

"I don't need your permission anymore. She invited me herself." Her phone dinged with another message. "She calls you the ghost man."

"Who is this girl?" Bailey asked again.

"Ah, she wants me to tell you she saw Thomas again last night."

Rand halted. "Really?"

Libby froze too, sensing her father's sudden change. "Yeah. See?" She held her phone toward Rand. He took it and read the message.

Tell your dad I saw Thomas last night.

"Who is Thomas?" Libby asked. Then comprehension dawned on her face. "Is that her ghost?"

"Yeah," Rand said, handing the phone back. As soon as they finished hiking, he'd ride over to St. Mary's and retrieve the recorder.

"Is this one of those haunting things you do, Mr. Rand?" Bailey asked. She waved her hands at him. "I don't want to hear about it. Your stories always keep me up at night." She trudged off down the trail.

"Is she okay?" Libby asked, squinting in the bright sunlight. "I mean... is Thomas a good ghost?"

"That's what I need to find out."

Something struck Rand hard on the cheek, just underneath his left eye, and he flinched. The rock that had hit him, about the size of a quarter, landed at his feet. "Ow!" He brought his hand up to the painful spot and felt warm blood trickle down his fingers.

"What the hell? Someone just threw a rock at you," Libby said. They both looked in the direction it had flown from.

They were alone on the trail.

Rand inspected the red on his fingertips.

"Where did that come from?" Libby asked. "That looks bad."

Rand looked around again, but there was definitely no one else in the area. Strange, since it felt like the rock was thrown from close range.

"Do you think it's one of those weird things that happen to you when you're doing a case?" Libby asked.

"Come on," Rand said, ignoring her. "Let's finish the trail."

AROUND ONE O'CLOCK, Rand pulled up in front of the huge house that belonged to Tessa's new fiancé, Bill. Rand hated going there, but Libby and Bailey were going to stay with the couple for the rest of the weekend, so he had to drop them off.

"Dad, your face is still bleeding," Libby said. "Come inside and put something on it."

"I'm fine."

"Don't be like that. Come on!"

"I don't want to go in there."

"It's a nice place, not a torture chamber." Libby yanked on his arm as she opened the car door. Rand sighed and killed the engine.

Tessa greeted them on the porch before they could finish crossing the huge front lawn. When she saw Rand approaching, her arms crossed and her expression grew dark.

"What's going on?" she asked.

"Someone threw a rock at Dad and he needs help."

"And why would anyone want to throw a rock at you, Randolph?" Tessa smiled.

"Hilarious."

"Let me see." Tessa grabbed Rand's wrist and forced his hand away from the cut. He felt the sticky blood all down his cheek, and the gash still pained him.

"Yeah, that's bad," Tessa said. "Come on. I have some alcohol inside."

"The medical kind or the drinking kind?" Rand said. Tessa gave him a look. "You don't have to do this," he added.

"Trust me, I know."

Rand had never been inside Bill's house before. He'd purposely avoided it. The man's living room was the size of Rand's entire home. Tessa sat him on a plush couch he would have happily slept on every night if he owned it.

Tessa returned a minute later with a bottle of rubbing alcohol, bandages, and a wet cloth. The cut stung as she cleaned it.

"Quit being a baby," she said.

"I didn't wince at all."

"You wanted to."

"Hey, did you know Libby has a boyfriend?"

"Justin. Yeah, he's a nice kid."

"You've met him?"

"Of course."

"Why did I not even know about him until today?"

"Because she knows you won't get along with her boyfriends."

"That's not the point," Rand said. "He's a dweeb."

Tessa applied the bandage to his face. "And this is why she hasn't introduced the two of you."

"And he pretends to play guitar just to get girls. I can't believe that worked on Libby. She's too smart for that."

"I admit, he's a bit weird, but he's good for Libby right now."

"What is that supposed to mean?"

Tessa used the wet rag to wipe the dried blood from Rand's cheek. The giant diamond engagement ring that Bill had given her threatened to give him a new cut. "It means we need to keep her dating him as long as possible. Because eventually she'll break up with him and date some bad boy to overcompensate."

"Why do you think that?"

"Because that's exactly what I did when I met you."

"I was *not* a bad boy."

Tessa snorted. "Motorcycle, no money, didn't care about anything."

"That was before the ghosts."

"Now you're just a haunted, semi-reformed bad boy. Don't worry, I found my happy medium."

"Bill is not a happy medium. He's an even bigger dweeb than Justin."

Tessa slapped his shoulder. "Rand, you don't even know him."

"I know the type. Come on."

Just then, Bill appeared at the entrance of the living room. He wore a white tennis outfit with shorts Rand considered far too short and a visor wrapped around his balding head. "Oh. Hi, Rand." His body grew rigid and nervous.

Rand nodded at him. "Bill."

"I'm going to go hit some balls with Frank," Bill said.

"Okay. Have fun," Tessa said.

Bill shuffled out the front door.

"I bet he likes hitting balls," Rand said.

"Shut up. I'm done, so you can leave now."

"You think he heard me earlier?"

"Rand. It's time for you to go."

Rand stood and ran his fingertips over the bandage on his face. "Nice patchwork, Tess."

"You're welcome."

"By the way, remember when I slipped on Adam's Peak in Sri Lanka? Gashed my thigh open from here to here, and no one was around for miles?"

"Yeah, yeah," Tessa said, "you don't need me or anyone else to fix you up. But it makes Libby happy to see it. That's the only reason I do it."

"Not the only reason." He smirked.

She shuffled him toward the front door. "Goodbye, Rand."

"Tell Libby to bring that guy over to my house next week. I have some questions for him."

"Sure thing, Rand." Tessa's tone was flat as she shut the door behind him.

Rand normally would have had no problem lingering a few more minutes to agitate his ex, but Georgia Collins returned to his mind, and the recorder underneath her bed that hopefully contained all the answers he needed.

9

Back at the hospital, Rand went to the tenth floor and greeted Harold. The guard smiled wide and shook his hand.

"How's everything going today, Harold?" Rand asked.

"It's a blessed day," he said. "Here to see Miss Georgia?"

"I am." Rand signed the paper in the binder and Harold gave him a nametag sticker. This time, he only wrote "RAND" on it.

"She's a sweetheart," Harold said, still smiling. "One of the best kids who's come through here. Shame about the condition she's in."

"I agree," Rand said. "Do you spend much time with the children, Harold?"

"I do when I can get away from my post," he said. "I have an open-desk policy around here." He leaned over and opened a big drawer in a filing cabinet behind him. Inside was an assortment of candy and toys. "For the younger ones."

Rand wondered if Harold was this friendly with all the

visitors. He also wondered if he knew about Georgia's little paranormal problem.

"Lucky kids," Rand said. "Maybe I'll take advantage of that open-desk policy myself."

Harold laughed. "Be my guest."

Rand found Nick and Maria in the room, huddled together on the couch and reading something on an iPad. The television was on the news channel and muted. Georgia was not there. A chair propped open the door, but Rand knocked on the doorframe anyway.

Nick and Maria looked up and smiled when they saw him.

"Come in," Maria said, standing. Nick joined her.

"Good afternoon," he said, as he walked in. He glanced around the room, but Georgia was gone.

"She stepped out," Nick told him.

Rand bent down and snatched the recorder from underneath Georgia's bed. The battery signal flashed red, but it was still on. He pressed the button, turned it off, and slipped it into his jacket pocket just as Georgia appeared in the doorway, rolling her oxygen tank behind her.

"Hey, it's the ghost man," she said, smiling. She removed her big sunglasses. "You'll never guess who I've been talking to."

"Libby already told me," Rand said.

"She seems cool. We're going to hang out soon."

"Libby is my daughter," Rand told Maria, who seemed confused by the conversation.

"Oh. How old is she?"

"Sixteen."

"What happened to you?" Georgia asked. She stared at the bandage on his cheek.

"Little hiking accident. No big deal."

"You used your face to break your fall?"

Rand laughed. "Something like that."

"Hey, you know Bonnie, the nurse?"

"No. Haven't met her."

"When we walked by the nurse's station yesterday and we waved, there were three there, right? Do you remember the one with the red hair?"

Rand hadn't been paying attention. "No, I don't."

"Oh. Well, she asked me about you. She thinks you're cute. You should get her number."

"Ah, I see. I'm actually already seeing someone."

"I won't tell her that," Georgia said. "I don't like to break hearts." She unhooked her tubing from her portable cylinder and attached the end of the tube to the fixture on the wall. "If you want to hang out again, just give me some time. I need to rest." Georgia's breath was quick, as if she'd been jogging.

"Take a breather, then," Rand said. "I have to step out and make a phone call anyway."

"Sure thing, Ghost Man." Georgia settled in and grabbed her laptop from the foot of the bed.

Rand went back into the hallway and Nick followed him. Nick kicked the chair away and let the hospital door fall into place.

"Is there somewhere private I can listen to this?" Rand asked, patting his pocket.

"There's a staff room at the end of the hall that doesn't get much use," Nick said. "You can try there. May I... come with you?"

"It's best if I listen alone first if you don't mind," Rand said. If there *were* otherworldly voices on the recorder, he didn't want to frighten his client. Besides, there was no telling what they would say.

"Right," Nick said. He already seemed afraid of what would be on there. "Georgia mentioned he came to her last night."

"Then let's hope we have something here."

"Break room is all the way at the end of the hall, on the left."

THE BREAK ROOM had a warm and musty odor to it. When Rand flipped the light switch—only one shimmered to life —he saw that the air vent had been closed. Inside, there was a round table with two chairs, an empty countertop, and a nonfunctioning refrigerator.

Rand slung his satchel off and took out his laptop. He connected the recorder and downloaded the file onto his desktop, then deleted the first hours of footage until he found the material recorded at night. It didn't take long before the audio line went flat, indicating that Georgia had gone to sleep.

Deep into the night, the line zigzagged to life. He placed his beginning point and clicked play.

He put on his large, noise-canceling headphones to listen closely.

It sounded like a distant whisper. He turned the volume on his computer all the way up and used his software to amplify the audio.

After listening to the garbled voice several times, he finally discerned words.

Wake up.

Rand's skin crawled. He had never gotten totally accustomed to hearing the voice of a spirit. The first contact always made him feel very uncomfortable.

Wake up, the voice said again.

There was definitely something visiting Georgia in the middle of the night.

There were long sections of silence. Rand's guess was that Georgia wasn't able to hear the ghost speaking to her. Voices of spirits traveled on different frequencies, which were sometimes difficult for human ears to pick up. They usually appeared much clearer on recordings.

Wake up.

Sounds of Georgia stirring awake crept into Rand's headphones. She most likely sensed the presence.

"Thomas." Georgia's voice was clear, although groggy with sleep and raspy as always. "Tell me what you want."

There was a long bout of silence.

"I can see you're trying to say something, but I don't hear anything," Georgia said.

Thomas spoke again, but Rand could not quite make out what was said.

"My parents think I'm crazy for saying you drop by at night," Georgia told Thomas. "But they brought in this guy. A ghost man. His name is Rand, and he's pretty cool. He's supposed to be some kind of expert."

And then Thomas responded, but this time he was louder. More agitated. Rand leaned in and paused the audio recording. The words had been unclear at first. He rewound the section and played it again, pressing the headphones into his ears and closing his eyes as he focused.

After listening three times, he thought he knew what the spirit was telling her.

Tell him to leave.

Rand leaned back in his chair and sighed. It looked like Thomas would not be that friendly toward him.

Georgia, of course, did not understand what he said. So she just kept going.

"I try to tell everyone it's fine that you come by. And that you don't hurt anything. By the way, are you ever going to do something besides stand in the corner? All you do is stare at me. It's kind of creepy, Thomas, to be honest."

Tell him to leave!

This time, the command was much more clear.

"And what do you want, anyway?" Georgia asked. She still couldn't hear Thomas. "Shouldn't you be free now? Why do you still want to hang around with CF kids? I'm guessing they don't have CF in the afterlife."

I want you to die.

Rand's breath caught.

"Does it hurt? Does it feel weird? Is there all the ice cream you could ever eat?"

I want you to die.

Thomas sounded angry when he said it. Rand was thankful Georgia couldn't hear the spirit.

"There isn't a lot of time left for me now," Georgia continued. "I realize that. But sometimes I wonder just how long I have left. And when my time comes, will I get to see you? Will I become a ghost like you? I hope not. I've been in this hospital room too much already."

Seventeen days.

Rand closed his eyes and buried his face in his hands. Georgia continued to talk to her friend in his headphones, but he heard nothing else she said.

Rand always taught in his classes to *never* ask spirits about future events. That always seemed to be the first thing people sought to learn when messing around with Ouija boards or other occult practices. And of all the milestones people most asked about—spouses, the number of children, wealth and health—the one thing that should never be asked is the hour of death.

Because these spirits knew. Time was not linear in the hereafter, so lingering presences were privy to future and past events in ways the living were not.

And if you asked about these events, they would happily tell you.

Tears burned in the corners of his eyes. This was why people were not meant to know the future. Rand felt like an intruder in Georgia's forthcoming life—her timeline, knowing something he shouldn't.

Thank God Georgia could not understand Thomas. She had not even directly asked, and still he had told her.

Although she had known this boy when he was alive, Rand knew the ghost was not a benign presence. He was bitter at having died young, jealous of Georgia still being alive, and he wanted her to join him in death. While Rand sympathized with the feelings the spirit had, they were not good for Georgia, and his rightful place was in the afterlife where he belonged.

Rand would have to remove Thomas and send him away. If he didn't, Thomas's presence would get stronger, and his voice clearer. Georgia would learn her fate sooner rather than later.

He'd had clients before who'd heard their day of death from spirits and remembered the madness they'd resorted to in order to change it. Ironically, knowing the end ruined whatever time they had left. Yet another reason why people were never meant to know.

Is it a threat instead of a premonition? Rand thought.

Meaning, would Thomas be the one to end her life in seventeen days? Or was he telling her that was when she would succumb to her condition?

Rand rewound the audio and listened again, but the spirit's meaning wasn't clear.

Rand swallowed the hard lump that had formed in his throat. Georgia's cystic fibrosis destined her for a short life, and no one knew exactly how much time she had left. Seventeen days could very well be accurate.

But if Thomas planned to cause her death in seventeen days, then Rand could save her by sending Thomas away.

He closed his laptop. He knew what he had to do—a cleansing ceremony inside Georgia's hospital room. That should force Thomas to move on to the afterlife.

And hopefully change the fate he'd promised Georgia.

10

R and composed himself and packed his equipment back into his satchel.

Although he had only met Georgia Collins yesterday, he was unnerved knowing that in seventeen days, she could possibly be gone.

And that he was the only one in the world who knew. Not even her doctors could predict it. This was when his line of work was especially difficult.

He returned to her hospital room. Nick and Maria looked up at him expectantly.

"Where's Georgia?" he asked.

"She went downstairs to get something to eat," Nick said. "Did the recording work?"

Rain pattered on the window. The storm had rolled in swiftly.

"Yes." He had to be careful with what he said here.

"And is everything all right?" Nick stood, rubbing his palms on his thighs as he did. "Is there actually a ghost?"

"Yes."

Nick and Maria exchanged a nervous look.

"Are you sure?" Nick asked, his skepticism peeking through.

"I heard it clearly on the recording," Rand said.

"So what will you do?"

"I'll remove it," Rand said. "Once he's sent away, he won't bother Georgia anymore."

And the sooner we do this, the better.

"What do you need from us?" Maria asked.

"Arrange for me to have some time alone in this room," Rand told her. "It won't take long."

"We can request to sign her out for a night and take her home," Maria said, glancing at Nick, who nodded. "This room can be all yours tomorrow evening."

"Can we do it tonight?" Rand asked.

"Um. I'll ask. I guess it would be okay."

"That would be perfect," Rand said. "I would still like to have a talk with Georgia about what's going on and what our plan is."

"She went down to the cafeteria," Nick said. "You can find her there."

"Good. While I'm gone, do whatever you need to sign Georgia out for the night."

WHEN RAND TOOK the elevator downstairs, he checked all around but did not spot Georgia. He found Mrs. Eloise at the register, and when he approached she looked at him over the top of her glasses.

"Well, if it isn't Miss Georgia's older man."

"Good afternoon, Mrs. Eloise," Rand said. "Have you seen Georgia? Her parents told me she was here."

"She just came through. Did you check outside?"

Rand went to the far side of the dining area. Although it was storming in full, he spotted Georgia sitting on a bench underneath an awning, watching the rain as it fell into the garden behind the cafeteria. Rand walked outside to join her.

She looked up when she sensed his presence over her shoulder. "Hey, Ghost Man."

"It's a wet one."

"Eh. I like it." She scooted to the left side of the bench, giving him room to sit. Her portable oxygen rested between her legs, and she was wearing her sunglasses again.

"Not feeling well?"

"Just weak today," she said. "It happens sometimes. Didn't get much sleep last night either."

"Thomas came to visit."

She looked at him. "How did you know?"

"You texted Libby and told her."

"Oh yeah."

"And… yesterday, I planted a recorder in your room."

Georgia removed her giant sunglasses. Her green eyes bored into him, and her expression was unreadable. Something between anger and surprise.

"You were spying on me, Ghost Man?"

"Not you. Thomas."

"I should be angrier about that, but I'm too curious about what you found out."

"I was able to pick up his end of the conversation you two had last night."

"Really?" Georgia twisted in the bench to face him, crossing her long, skinny legs. "You heard what he was saying?"

"Yes."

"That's great! Like I told you yesterday, I can always tell he's trying to say something, but I can't understand him."

"That's common," Rand said. "Their words are coming from another realm of existence, so it's hard for our human ears to pick up sometimes unless the presence is very strong. On a recording, it often comes through much clearer."

Georgia looked amazed. Even in awe. "This is such good news."

"How come?" Rand asked.

"Because… Okay, promise you won't tell my parents?"

He nodded.

"Good. I know I can trust you, Ghost Man. The truth is, I've come to terms with the whole dying young thing. I'm mostly over it, but that doesn't mean I don't have difficult moments sometimes."

"I get it," Rand said.

"Some days I'm still afraid to die. Some nights I can't sleep because I'm wondering what it feels like to be dead."

Seventeen days, Thomas's voice echoed in Rand's mind.

Georgia's face, usually so bright, had fallen. Her eyes drifted to the rainstorm. The plant leaves were battered by the falling drops.

"That's why I'm glad you came," she said. "I was hoping you could help me communicate with Thomas. Maybe he can answer some of my questions."

Rand watched her for a long time. He could sense her

uncertainty. He knew she was desperate to find reassurance from her friend.

Georgia looked at him again. "Can you help me, Ghost Man?"

Rand took a deep breath and let it out slowly. "I can. But not in the way you want."

Georgia frowned. "What do you mean?"

"I mean I could hear Thomas's side of the conversation. And it isn't what you would expect. Thomas is not happy. He's bitter. And from what I can tell, he's a little jealous that you're alive and he isn't."

Georgia furrowed her brow. "That doesn't sound like Thomas at all."

"That's the tricky thing with these ghosts. Sometimes when they come back, they aren't the same as they were when they were alive. Things change between life and death."

"Then we'll ask him what's wrong," Georgia said. "We need to reassure him. Or make him feel better. Or something."

Rand shook his head, and he could see Georgia's hopes getting dashed. "It's not that simple, Georgia. Spirits aren't like people, and we can't reason with them. They are trapped here because they feel their time on earth is unfinished, or they are not satisfied with how they lived their lives. They don't belong here, like you or I do."

"Then we need to help him," Georgia said.

"I agree. And the best way we can do that is to send him away."

Georgia's face dimmed, and Rand thought he could see tears welling in her eyes. He hated telling her what she didn't want to hear.

"What do you mean?" Georgia asked.

"I mean send him on to the afterlife. To where his spirit belongs."

"No," Georgia said. "We can't do that. I like him here."

"Why is that?"

"Because he was my best friend when he was alive and knowing he's looking out for me makes me feel better."

I want you to die.

"Georgia, he isn't looking out for you."

"How do you know?"

"Because I heard what he was telling you."

"And what did he say?"

Seventeen days.

"I can't tell you that."

"That's bullshit! I want to know."

"You don't," Rand said gently. "Trust me."

"What? Was he, like, cursing me out? Or telling me he always hated me?"

"No, nothing like that." *Much worse.*

"Then I don't understand."

"You need to trust me," Rand said. "I've encountered bitter ghosts before, and even though we think they're our loved ones, they're often not the same. The best place for them is the afterlife."

"I don't *want* him in the afterlife," Georgia protested. "I want him here. He's the only thing I have right now that makes me feel better about dying!" She finally broke, and the tears streamed down her face. "Having him here shows this isn't the end, and that even after I pass, I'll still be able to see my mom and dad." She sniffed, then wiped her nose with the back of her hand.

Rand was quiet for a few minutes and let Georgia cry.

He understood her point of view completely, but that was why it was so difficult. It was hard to make her understand why Thomas's presence wasn't good without telling her what he knew.

When she got her sobs under control, she looked up at him again. "I thought you were here to help me."

"I am. But sometimes help doesn't always look the way we want it to."

Georgia shook her head. "I can't believe it. I finally get a break, my friend coming back and showing me that dying isn't that bad. And now you want to take that away from me."

"Please try to understand," Rand said. "Thomas is not the same as before."

"Oh yeah? Prove it. Let me hear your recording."

"I won't do that."

"Then you're just some scammer. Maybe there isn't even anything on your recorder." She stood and grabbed her oxygen tank. "Thanks for nothing."

Then she stormed off.

Rand watched her go. Hurting her now reminded him of the times when Libby thought she knew best, and Rand had to tell her no. He hated to see his daughter upset but had to stand strong and not give in. That was true here as well.

Georgia's reason for wanting Thomas around was compelling, but Rand knew he had to do what was right.

11

Rand informed Nick and Maria Collins that he planned to remove the ghost using a cleansing ceremony. Although they both seemed a little skeptical, they were nevertheless on board with the idea.

They got clearance from the doctor to let Georgia spend the night at home, then they signed her out.

Rand had dinner in the St. Mary's cafeteria downstairs while he waited for the family to vacate, not wanting to be present. He knew Georgia would be very unhappy and not want to see him.

Around eight o'clock, Nick called him.

"Okay, we're home," he said.

"How did it go?" Rand asked.

"She was not pleased," Nick told him.

"I figured. I'm not her favorite person in the world right now. But trust me, this is for the best."

"I believe you. Do what you have to do."

Rand returned to the tenth floor, satchel dangling

from his shoulder. It was heavy with all the supplies he'd need.

Harold the security guard gave him a strange look as he passed the desk. "Mr. Rand? The Collins family has signed out of the hospital for the evening."

Rand froze. He still wore his visitor name tag, but it probably didn't have much authority when the patient he was registered as visiting wasn't even in the facility.

"Yeah," Rand said. A couple of likely lies popped into his head, but he found he couldn't be dishonest with the man.

Harold wrinkled his brow, confused. Rand knew this was the part where Harold would ask him to leave. But instead, Harold said, "May I have a word?"

Rand returned to the desk and let his satchel drop to the floor by his feet.

The robust man leaned forward and brought his face close to Rand's. "Miss Georgia tells me things. And she told me about you and what you're doing here." Although no one was in earshot, he kept his voice low.

Rand nodded. *So I was right. He does know more about this than he let on.*

"I was the first to know about her little friend coming to visit her in the middle of the night."

"I had a feeling you were a believer," Rand said.

Harold licked his lips and hesitated. Finally, he said, "I am. I've had a few unexplainable experiences in my life, but I try to leave well enough alone. I don't think any good can come from messing with this stuff."

"Wise man," Rand said. How he wished more people felt the same way as Harold. "But not everyone is as wary as you, and they can get themselves into serious trouble."

"A young lady like Miss Georgia has no business dabbling around with all this," Harold said.

"I agree."

"I hoped you weren't here to encourage her curiosity, but I didn't think so. I got a good feeling from you."

"And I from you. I'm here to get rid of it. That's why they took Georgia away for the night."

"Hospital policy says the visitors can't stay when the patient is gone."

"Smart policy," Rand said. "Give me an hour?"

Harold nodded his head. "Make it quick."

RAND PLACED candles around the empty hospital room and ignited them. Then he turned out the lights, leaving only an eerie darkness. He took out his incense and lit it, letting the scented smoke drift through the air. He removed his jacket and placed it on the couch.

He'd done cleansing ceremonies countless times, but to him, it would never be a matter of routine. Supernatural entities were far too unpredictable, and for that reason, Rand still got nervous when preparing for an encounter.

The storm from earlier had mostly passed, but the last remains of the thunder rolled in the distance.

Rand stood in the middle of the room and closed his eyes. Embraced the silence. Smelled the incense.

And felt he was not the only one in the room.

Rand was not a clairvoyant, but he had been around enough spiritual activity to recognize when it was present.

"You are here with me," he said out loud. Nothing replied. "I can sense you. Don't worry. I am not here to harm you."

More silence. Rand opened his eyes. He withdrew from his bag a small cross dangling from rosary beads. He held the thing high above his head, displaying it to the four corners of the room.

"It is time for you to move on from this place," Rand said.

A loud crash startled him. A picture frame—a photo of Georgia and three other young girls—had fallen off the wall and smashed on the ground.

Thomas would resist.

But the thing about the spiritual realm was that it had to listen to the commands of those who occupied the mortal plane. They didn't have to like it, but they had to obey.

"I know you can hear me," Rand said, looking around the room, speaking loudly and clearly. "You are loved and remembered here, and we have all grieved your loss. But it is time for you to walk toward the light where you belong. You will be happier there, and the ones you love will remember you fondly until it is time for you all to meet again."

The room's temperature suddenly grew very cold. The presence of a spirit consumed the heat from the room, which caused the room to become unnaturally cold all at once.

Two candles near Georgia's bed blew out at the same time.

"I know you don't want to go, but you must," Rand said.

A vase of flowers on Georgia's desk shifted by itself—Rand saw it just in time. It flew from the desk, right toward his head, but he dodged. It smashed on the opposite wall, sending flowers, glass, and water all over the floor.

This one is strong, Rand thought. Stronger than he'd originally thought. He was right in figuring he needed to cleanse the room immediately.

"I command you to leave this place!" Rand said, voice booming. When the spirits were stubborn, he had to be especially firm. "Walk toward the light! Embrace the next life. You are not welcome here, and you will come here no more!"

The bathroom door swung open and closed by itself, slamming shut. The television turned on, though it displayed nothing but static. Georgia's desk drawers opened and the pens, pencils, and papers inside flew around the room.

It's trying to throw me off.

"Georgia does not need you anymore!" Rand shouted. "You do not belong. I command you to leave this place!"

The doors and drawers stopped moving on their own and the objects being thrown around came to rest on the floor. The tension in the room eased and evaporated, and the temperature slowly returned to normal. Static on the TV was the only sound.

And then, after a few seconds, Rand took a deep breath and lowered the rosary beads. He closed his eyes and felt out the space for a few moments, to confirm that he was alone.

The room felt empty. Lighter, even.

The spirit was gone.

But it was too easy.

A little voice in the back of Rand's head told him it shouldn't have been that simple. The ghost was stronger than he'd expected, so Rand lingered a few seconds longer to confirm that he'd been successful. He sensed nothing out of the ordinary.

There is no presence here any longer, Rand told himself.

Rand blew out the candles and packed his things. He did his best to clean up the mess Thomas had made—throwing away the pieces of the broken vase and putting the pens and pencils back in the drawers. He threw his bag over his shoulder and checked his watch. The hour that Harold had given him was almost up.

He opened the door, and as he went to step out into the hallway he took one last look over his shoulder. Scanned the room from wall to wall, glancing into the four corners.

Definitely gone. No spirit before had ever withstood one of his cleansing ceremonies.

Thomas was no different.

12

I t took Libby fifteen minutes to find the correct elevator. She could imagine her dad getting hopelessly lost in this hospital.

And he would never tell me if he did.

The doors opened on the tenth floor and Libby stepped out, looking around. The ward now made her feel like she was in a hospital for the first time. Hospitals gave her dad the creeps, but she didn't mind them. When she was younger, she had done some volunteer work at St. Mary's with her mom.

The security guard stood as she approached, giving her a broad smile. "Good evening, ma'am."

"Hello," Libby said. "I'm here to visit Georgia Collins."

"Certainly." The guard produced a binder and opened it for her, where Libby signed her name. She checked her cheap digital watch and filled in the time—5:50 PM.

The guard took the binder back and copied her name onto a nametag. He smirked as he did. "Any relation to a Randolph?"

Libby winced. "Are you going to throw me out?"

He laughed. "I like him. Haven't seen him in a while, though." The guard—whose badge read Harold—flipped a few pages back and ran his finger down the boxes. "Ten days ago."

"Yeah. He's been busy." Libby peeled the sticker off and smoothed it onto her shirt. "I'm his daughter."

"Welcome to the tenth ward. I'm Harold, the security guard up here. Room 1019 is down that way and on the right."

Libby thanked him and made her way past the nurse station and down the hall. She found the door of 1019 wide open. The girl whose Instagram she'd been following the last week and a half was propped on her bed, watching television. The nasal cannula that was always in her pictures hung from her nose.

Libby scanned the hospital room, which resembled a normal bedroom. "I like what you've done with the place."

Georgia noticed her for the first time, smiled, and stood. Without saying anything, she opened her arms wide for a hug, and Libby scooped her up.

"Thank you for coming," Georgia said.

"Absolutely. I heard the ice cream here is amazing." They sat down together on the bed. "Seriously," Libby said, looking around. "This place looks incredible. So comfortable."

"Basically, I moved in," Georgia said. "No idea what the rent is, but my parents tell me it isn't cheap."

"I wanted to paint the walls in my bedroom at my dad's house," Libby said. "I like blue, but right now it's white, which is what it was when he bought the place. But he told me no. Said I'd make too much of a mess and that I didn't know what I was doing."

"*Do* you know what you're doing, though?" Georgia asked. "Do you actually know how to paint a room?"

"Of course not," Libby said. "But I wanted to try."

Georgia chuckled. "You should just do it anyway. Who cares?"

"You're right," Libby said. "He never goes in there. We can make bets on how long it'll take him to notice. Maybe three months?"

"How is the ghost man?" Georgia asked, her voice flat.

"Fine. Busy teaching. Out with his girlfriend. Stuff like that."

Georgia grunted.

Her dad had told her what had gone down with the ghost. In the end, he'd ended up having to remove it, and Georgia was upset with him about that. It had been a tough call, Libby realized. But Libby knew enough about these ghosts to know it was the right thing to do.

"I like your clothes," Georgia said, her eyes scanning her up and down. "You play volleyball?"

"Oh, this. Sorry, I just came from practice."

"No, that's awesome. Sometimes I watch it on TV. It looks like so much fun."

"Have you ever played?"

"No way. Look at me, I can't even breathe."

"Come with me sometime. We'll hit some balls."

Georgia straightened. "Are you serious?"

"Of course."

"That would be great."

"So what about you?" Libby asked. "What do you do when you're here?" As soon as the words left her mouth, she regretted it. There couldn't be too many interesting things to do in a hospital.

But Georgia only perked up. "This place is so huge. I explore and get into places where I'm not supposed to."

"Oh yeah? Like where?" Libby instantly considered the morgue and hoped that wasn't what she meant.

"You want to see my secret spot?" Georgia asked her. "I didn't even show your dad."

"Absolutely."

"Okay." She nodded toward Libby's gym bag from volleyball practice that she still had. "Bring your gear."

———

ON THE ELEVATOR, Georgia pressed the button for 15R, which was located between floors fourteen and fifteen.

"I like your bag," Libby said as they rode. Georgia had a nice, heavy-duty carrier for her tanks that had lots of little pockets.

"I'll get you one for Christmas. Oxygen not included."

The elevator opened into an area that they clearly were not supposed to be in. It was not a normal ward, but rather a long hallway that still looked like it was undergoing construction. The walls were wood, not painted, and the nice tile that finished the floor in other parts of the hospital was not there. It was also very warm and humid.

But Georgia led the way confidently, pulling her tank on wheels behind her.

At the end of the hall was a small security station with a man wearing the same uniform as Harold. He stood as they approached. At first, Libby noted that he looked concerned and confrontational, but when he saw Georgia, he softened.

"I told you not to come back, Georgia," the guard said. "You're going to get me in trouble."

"How? I'm literally the best secret keeper ever."

"I know, but it's only a matter of time. If Ms. Shaw figures this out, I'm done for."

"I'll take the fall for you, Sam."

Sam glanced at Libby. "Does she keep *your* secrets?"

"Every last one," Libby answered. Georgia smiled at her.

Sam waved them through. "Okay. Make it quick."

"Yes! Thanks, Sam!"

Georgia tugged Libby's arm and pulled her past the security desk toward a set of double doors. "No one can say no to me," she whispered to Libby.

When the doors opened, a blast of chilly wind hit Libby in the face. The dark hallway disappeared, and they walked outside onto the roof of the hospital. The sounds of the city at rush hour came from far below them, and the sky was orange and purple as the sun fell on the distant horizon.

"Oh my God," Libby said. When she looked up, the rest of St. Mary's fifteen floors towered above her and the platform they were on, making her feel tiny. On the ground was a huge H surrounded by a white circle.

"Pretty amazing, right?" Georgia said.

"Yes. This is awesome!"

Libby took her volleyball from her gym bag and dribbled it. "Want to hit a few?"

"Are you serious? Yes!"

"Do you know how to do it?" Libby tossed the ball in the air and then bounced it off her arms for a few rounds.

"I've seen games on TV," Georgia said. She mimicked Libby with her hand position, and Libby went to her and corrected her placement, folding them correctly to give her a sturdy landing point for the ball.

"Get under it, bend your knees, and focus on where you want the ball to go. You don't need to hit it very hard to have a lot of power. Let's try."

Libby lobbed her the ball, slow and easy and from a short distance. Georgia sent it sailing up in the air with a loud slap from her pale forearms. Libby ran and caught it. The heavy wind around the helipad had taken it off center. "Very nice. Have you done this before?"

Georgia shrugged and smirked.

Libby volleyed it to her again, and Georgia hit it back, this time more controlled and accounting for the wind. Libby returned it to her, and Georgia responded. They went back and forth before Georgia finally dropped it.

"You're so lucky you get to do this," Georgia said, picking up the volleyball before it rolled away.

"You can do it too." Libby hoped to be encouraging, but really had no idea of Georgia's limitations with her condition.

Georgia said nothing, only served the ball to Libby, which she bumped, set, and volleyed back.

They bounced it between themselves, controlled and easy. "See! You're doing it," Libby said. "You could totally do this in a real game."

Libby's next volley was stronger than she'd intended and was swept up by the wind, and Georgia scrambled to get under it. But her oxygen tubing ran out of slack, yanked her face back, and popped out of her nostrils. The tug caused the portable cylinder to fall over, and even though it was in a padded carrying bag it made a loud clank on the concrete.

Libby rushed over, but she relaxed when she saw Georgia smiling.

"I need to commission some longer tubing," she said, stringing the cannula back behind her ears and returning them to her nostrils, panting as if she'd just run a half marathon. She put the portable cylinder right-side-up.

"Let's take a break." Libby was shocked by how quickly the other girl ran out of breath.

"I'm totally jealous of you," Georgia said, placing her hands on her hips to catch her breath. "You're tall, pretty, athletic. You have a cool dad, even though I'm mad at him right now. You probably have a boyfriend."

Libby smirked. "I like you, too."

"You still wouldn't want to trade places with me. I wouldn't let you. What's your boyfriend's name?"

"Justin. Although he isn't my boyfriend yet. We're just kind of texting."

"Lock him down!" Georgia said. "God, I wish I had a boyfriend."

"There's never any rush for a boyfriend," Libby said. "I never thought I wanted one, but then I met Justin and things are just kind of happening."

"I have a legitimate reason for rushing to get a boyfriend," Georgia said, and Libby fell silent. "Do you believe in all the stuff that your dad is involved in?"

"Of course." Libby was glad for the change of topic. "It's hard not to. I've grown up around it my whole life."

Georgia pulled her oxygen along as she walked down

the helipad and scooped up the ball. Libby followed her to the edge of the platform, and the heights made her start to feel woozy. Georgia seemed unafraid.

"Did he tell you about me? And my situation?" Libby nodded. "What do you think about it?"

Libby looked away. The streetlights below were twinkling to life with the setting sun. Car horns and the sounds of roaring engines floated up from the rush-hour traffic. Libby took a deep breath, and somehow the air seemed clearer up there. Perhaps that was why Georgia visited. "He did the right thing."

Georgia frowned and tucked a piece of hair behind her ear, and the wind tugged it out of place again. "I miss my friend."

"I know you do." She paused. "Does that mean you haven't seen him since my dad was here?"

"He's gone."

Good, Libby thought. "I know it's hard, but sometimes it isn't a good thing when these two worlds come together." *Oh God, I sound like my dad.*

"I didn't think he was hurting anyone," Georgia said.

"Maybe not at first. But who knows what can happen later?" Libby remembered several of her father's cases that had begun as a benign presence and then escalated. Most people only waited to contact him after things had taken a turn for the worst. Georgia and her family had been lucky. "Can you forgive him?"

Georgia shrugged. "I'm already kind of over it. But still. I miss Thomas."

Libby put her hands on Georgia's shoulders and forced the girl to look her in the eyes. "No one is saying you can't miss Thomas. But it is way better if you stay in the present moment. Focus on life. Not on death."

Georgia's face broke into a smile. Then she nodded. "Okay."

"Promise me."

"Yes, I will."

"Good. I can already tell you're stronger than a lot of the girls in my class. *And* you have your very own helipad. Let's get a selfie because this needs to go on Instagram."

They spent ten minutes finding the perfect angle for the helipad, the sunset, and their faces. Eighty pictures later, Sam came outside. "Just got a call on the radio. Chopper coming in. Bad accident on the Interstate."

Georgia tossed him the volleyball, which he caught easily. "You kicking us out?"

"Do you want to get crushed?" Sam dribbled the ball between his legs as if it were a basketball.

"There are some good ones in here," Libby said, scrolling through her camera roll. "Do you mind if I post them?"

"Is that a serious question?"

13

Georgia tried the chord progression again, but the last one strummed awkward and flat. She groaned and rewound the YouTube video on her laptop.

The girl in the video demonstrated again, and Georgia watched closely. Eventually, she saw what she was doing wrong with the last chord.

Georgia paused the video again and strummed her guitar a few more times, and finally it sounded right. As she repeated the chords over and over, she added in lyrics, singing them underneath her breath.

Singing was hard to do with lungs filled with muck and oxygen running through her nose, but she didn't care. She liked to sing, so she was going to.

Three knocks interrupted her song just as it was coming along. The door opened and Nurse Donna appeared.

"Evening, Georgia," she said.

"Hey there." Georgia twisted in her chair to face the other woman.

"Where's your mom and dad?"

"They went out to eat. They'll be back later."

"Ah, okay. Well, we have a cake out here for Mandy's birthday."

"What kind?"

"Red velvet."

"Mmm. That'll do. Yeah, I'll be there in a minute. Going to rock out for a little longer while I have the room to myself."

Donna smiled. "Sure thing. It'll be at the nurse's station whenever you want it." She left the door open and walked away.

Georgia returned to her guitar. After playing through the first verse and singing along a couple of times, she figured she had it down. She fast-forwarded the YouTube video to the part that would teach her the chorus.

Another three knocks.

"Yeah, just a few minutes more," Georgia said, keeping her eyes on her laptop. "Don't tell me y'all ate all the cake already."

But when she looked toward the door, no one was there.

"Mrs. Donna?" Georgia called.

No answer.

Georgia turned back to her computer and played the video. The girl used a close-up of her fingers to outline the chord progression for the chorus.

A loud slam startled Georgia and made her jump.

She whirled around. The door was closed.

"Mrs. Donna?" she said again, her voice trembling

from the sudden fright. She leaned her guitar against her desk and rose from the chair, pulling her oxygen cylinder behind her as she slowly approached the door that had been open moments before.

She tried to open it, but it wouldn't. Hospital doors didn't lock, so it was like someone was holding it closed from the other side.

"Hey!" she shouted, slamming her palm against the wood.

But all the exertion had left her short of breath, and she felt a coughing fit coming on. Georgia backed away and focused on getting her breathing under control. Her coughing fits could last up to fifteen minutes sometimes, and her parents were due back any minute. If they found her coughing, they'd worry about her the rest of the night.

Her breath leveled off. She readjusted the cannula in her nose and felt the pure oxygen filling her lungs.

Then she went to the bed and pressed the Call button on the wall.

Nothing.

Usually it beeped and lit up red. Georgia mashed it a few more times, but it wasn't working.

She then went to the bathroom and pulled on the Call cord that dangled above her toilet. Still nothing.

"What's going on?" she whispered to herself.

Her cell phone was on the bed, plugged into the charger. She was sure she had the number for the nurse station saved in her contacts.

But she stopped short as her room filled with music.

At first, she thought the YouTube video had unpaused itself, but when she looked at her desk she saw it was her guitar.

Playing itself.

The strings pressed down on the frets in flawless chords and strummed, creating a full sound. It was the song she'd been trying to learn. Executed perfectly.

Georgia stared at the instrument, mouth open in awe. And a tightening ball of anxiety began to form in her stomach.

Then, an unmistakable soft breath on the back of her neck.

She whirled around, her hand instinctively going to where the breath had been. But no one was behind her.

"Thomas?" she said, voice trembling.

The song ended with a jarring, dissonant chord and fell silent.

Thomas had played guitar. It would make sense if it were him. *But I thought Ghost Man got rid of him.*

"Is that you?" The only sound in the room now was Georgia's breath. Her pulse rang in her ears. "Please tell me you're still here. Give me a sign or something."

As if on command, the green oxygen cylinder by her bed fell over, landing with a loud clang. The top then burst off, white smoke shooting from the broken handle. The compressed air sent the tank flying across the floor with the speed and force of a torpedo, right toward Georgia's ankles. She leapt out of the way just in time. It crashed into the wall, leaving a spider web of cracks in the plaster. The television toppled off its stand and dropped to the ground, and the wires were yanked from the electrical sockets.

Georgia cried out. Her breath turned to rapid pants, and she was no longer able to control it.

"Thomas! What are you doing?"

The oxygen cylinder by her side was knocked over, the top popping open by itself, just like the first one. It shot across the room, ripping the cannula from her nose as it went. The force was strong enough to pull her off her feet and she face-planted onto the floor. The rogue cylinder crashed against the door and spun in circles as the last of the air inside leaked out.

She coughed and sputtered, a heaviness in her chest cutting off her breath. And there were no more tanks in the room.

"Thomas," she wheezed. "I'm sorry. I didn't want—" She crawled toward her bed, desperate for her phone.

She reached the foot of the bed, breathless, and fumbled blindly across the mattress for her cell.

As soon as she grabbed it, the lights in the room went out.

She whirled around, back propped against her bed, coughing and hacking. It was completely dark inside—even her laptop had shut off by itself. The room was suddenly very cold, frigid as if she'd walked into a freezer.

"I'm sorry," she said again.

She understood if Thomas was angry for being sent away. But surely he realized it wasn't her idea. Didn't he?

Then, something caught her eye. Although it was dark, she could make out the outline of a figure standing in the corner of the room. A person. A boy.

Thomas.

It had been a little over a week since she'd seen him. He stood still and stared at her, even though his features were not clear. Somehow, his shadow was blacker than the surrounding darkness, allowing him to stand out.

She pointed her phone toward the figure and opened

her camera app, then pressed the button. The flash went off, blinding her.

As soon as the light faded, Thomas was inches away, having crossed the room in a millisecond to stand over her.

Georgia clenched her eyes shut, covered her ears, and screamed, waiting for whatever Thomas was going to do to her. However, he would punish her.

But then familiar arms were around her. She opened her eyes. The lights were back and her parents were there. Her mom held her close.

"What happened?" she asked. "Why are you screaming?"

Georgia didn't answer. Instead, she only patted her chest, coughing and wheezing. Her dad looked around the room and, finding both tanks empty, ran out into the hallway and shouted for the nurses to bring oxygen.

Nurse Donna and others rushed in, picked her up, and put her on the bed, then reattached her oxygen and tried to calm her down.

As she sucked down the oxygen, Georgia's eyes darted around the room, looking for Thomas. She knew he was still there somewhere, unseen and invisible, hiding from everyone else who had come into the room.

Waiting for the next time she would be alone.

14

It was a Friday morning and Rand drummed his fingers on the steering wheel as he sang along with a Motley Crüe song on the classic rock radio station. It had been ten days since he'd seen Georgia Collins, but she still lingered on his mind.

He ran into the dry cleaners and gave the girl his ticket. She then retrieved his black suit, which was on a velvet hanger and covered in plastic. Rand thanked her and went to Vicky's Alterations down the road. There, he put on the suit and stood in front of a mirror as she measured him and put the pins in the coat and waistline.

"Everything's tighter," she said around the sharp needles in her mouth.

"I've taken up weightlifting the past couple of years." He'd bulked up since the last time he'd worn the suit, especially his thighs. Squats were a killer.

"When do you need this by?" Vicky asked him.

"By tonight. I have a thing."

She glanced up at him. "You know I'm a twenty-four-hour turnaround."

"Do you have an express option?"

She sighed. "I'll do it for you this time, Rand. But don't get used to it."

"I already am."

The next stop was the gym. It was leg day, so he loaded up a heavy barbell on his back and squatted, face red and forehead sweaty, while his headphones blared Motörhead. When the squats were done, he waddled over to the gym's pool, changed into swim trunks, and did some laps.

After he showered, he checked his phone and found a message from Vicky. The suit was finished, so he swung by and picked it up again.

That evening, however, he dressed in his navy blue suit.

He slung the jacket over his white shirt, which he left unbuttoned at the top. Rachel came into the bedroom from the bathroom, her salmon dress tightly hugging her body. She tilted her head as she put on her earring. "I thought you were wearing black tonight."

"Changed my mind."

"After all that? Dry cleaning and tailoring?"

"It needed to be done anyway."

"No tie?"

"Ties are too uptight."

"You'll be the only man without one."

"I'm aware."

At six o'clock, they went to the car.

"Thanks again for coming with me," Rand said as they got in.

"Still a little weird," Rachel told him.

"I know. Don't worry, we won't stay long." He started the engine. The classic rock station from earlier blared too loud, and he twisted the volume knob as Rachel cringed.

"But we can't leave too early. They'll notice," Rachel said.

"If they're noticing my whereabouts at their own celebration, then they don't know how to party."

She smirked as they backed out of the driveway.

Preston Plantation was a manor outside of town surrounded by several acres of land dotted by hundred-year-old oak trees. Like most plantations in the south, it was now used as an indoor reception hall.

Rand parked, and as they walked toward the main building he noticed that, in fact, he was the only one not wearing a tie. He also sensed the heavy feeling within the walls of Preston Plantation. It was an old home, and therefore likely haunted. Wealthy families would have lived there, and usually, they had their fair share of problems, debauchery, and mistreated servants. Plenty of negative energy to attract lingering spirits.

"What's wrong?" Rachel asked. She'd noticed him glancing up at the high ceilings and toward the corners of the room, and at the portraits of the past owners that adorned the wall along the staircase that led up to a darkened, unused second floor.

"Nothing," Rand said, pushing the thoughts from his mind.

He'd attended engagement parties before, but none that resembled an actual wedding. Bill had spared no expense, as usual. The main reception hall was decked out for the occasion, with pink tablecloths matching the curtains of the high windows. A live band played slow songs on their woodwind instruments, which Rand hardly thought was useful if one were trying to throw a decent party, but to each their own. He swung by all the offerings—the roast carvery, the vegetables, the lobster tails, pasta, and even the children's chicken finger stand. Last, but not least, was the open bar.

"I've never seen you eat so much," Rachel told him. Three empty plates had accumulated in front of him before a busboy came to clear them.

"Bill's dollar, so why not?" He leaned in his chair and sipped his whiskey.

They sat alone at a table in the back, separate from the main party. Well aware that he was only there as Libby's father, he kept away and let the others do their thing. Tessa and Bill floated from conversation to conversation, playing host. Libby stood in a huddle with her friends Bailey, Claire, and Samantha. Libby wore a red dress that Rand had never seen before. Justin was with her, looking awkward in his oversized suit, hands in his pockets, seeming like he didn't have much to say to the girls.

"Thoughtful of Bill to let Libby invite her friends," Rand said. Despite Bill being able to afford the extra heads at a dinner like that, there were still a lot of empty seats in the place. Just like Rand's classroom.

"He really is a nice guy," Rachel said. She signaled for the waiter, who swooped in and placed another champagne on the table in front of her, and took away her empty glass. By Rand's count, she was three deep.

"When have you ever talked to Bill?"

"He came by when you were in the bathroom."

Rand smirked. "That rat."

Rachel shoved his shoulder.

Tessa caught his eye again for the fifth time that night. She looked stunning in her blue dress, and the personal trainer that Bill had gotten her for her most recent birthday was really starting to pay off.

In a locked container at the back of his closet, there was a ring in a little black box. No one else knew it was there. He'd bought it years ago and had held on to it ever since. Soon after Libby was born Tessa had made it clear she had no intention of being with him long term, so Rand had never actually asked Tessa to marry him. And even though money had been tight, he'd never sold it.

He drained his whiskey. "Think I'll hit the bar again. Want anything?" Rachel shook her head and nodded toward her full champagne. "And on the way back, I think it's time I meet my daughter's new boyfriend."

"Be nice, Randolph."

"Aren't I always?"

She gave him a look as he rose.

Rand tipped the bartender and carried his whiskey glass to where his daughter and her friends stood. Libby's eyes widened when he approached.

"Evening," he said as he broke into their circle. Bailey and Claire made room for him.

"Hey, Mr. Rand," Bailey said.

"How's the party so far?"

"Music's terrible." Bailey wrinkled her nose at the four old guys on the stage.

"You know, I was just telling Rachel the same thing."

"Right? A DJ would have been much better. And cheaper."

"Money isn't an issue in a crowd like this, Bailey. And look around at these people. I doubt they've ever heard a DJ before."

The party was mostly made up of what Rand assumed were Bill's work colleagues. Everyone wore a stiff, unfitted suit, and conducted themselves as if they were there for business rather than a celebration. Hunched shoulders, serious expressions, and formal head nods.

Rand then focused on Justin and extended his hand. "Rand Casey."

Justin awkwardly shook it, his hand limp like a dead fish. "Justin."

Libby folded her arms and glared at her father with a stiff-lipped warning, which Rand already intended to ignore.

"Libby's dad."

"I know," Justin said. His eyes darted around the floor at everyone's ankles.

"Nice suit. I have one just like it. I'll give you my tailor's number. Tell her I sent you and you'll have it back same day."

"Dad," Libby spat.

"Thanks," Justin said, missing the gentle jibe.

Bailey and Claire stood tensed on either side of him, awkwardly watching a father meet a boyfriend for the first time.

"So I hear you play guitar."

"A little." He ran a nervous hand through his shaggy, unkempt hair.

"Weren't you supposed to wear your black suit tonight?" Libby asked, desperately trying to change the conversation.

"A little? What does that mean? You either do or you don't. What kind of music do you play?"

"Mostly original stuff."

"I'd love to hear it sometime. You know, I used to play a bit myself."

"Dad," Libby said again.

"I was in a band in college," Rand went on. "We played at the bars every weekend. There were four of us, and we called ourselves Amateur Surgery." Rand chuckled, lost in the memory. "Man, we thought we were awesome, but really all we wanted to do was make as much noise as possible. The ladies loved us, though."

"Dad!"

Rand turned toward Libby. She gripped her cell phone, a look of concern on her face. "What?"

"I just got a text from Georgia."

Rand frowned. "Saying what?"

"He's back." The words were a whisper barely audible over the band's interlude. She passed him her phone, and the latest message in their thread was a picture. Rand swallowed.

He recognized the hospital room. And in the darkened shadows, on the edge of the flash from the phone's camera, he could make out the spectral outline of a boy standing in the corner.

It was their first photograph of Thomas. This meant that not only was he back, but his presence was stronger.

"Oh no," he muttered.

Justin and Libby's friends looked back and forth between them, confused.

His own phone vibrated with a call in his pocket. When he fished it out, Nick Collins's name was on the screen.

"Excuse me," he told the kids. "I need to take this."

15

St. Mary's Hospital was just as busy at night as it was in the morning.

Rand, Libby, and Rachel approached the Coffee Bean, the same shop where Rand had originally met up with Nick and Maria.

Maria was waiting for them and stood when they neared.

"Oh, I'm so sorry," she said when she saw how they were dressed. "You should have told me you had plans."

"It's okay," Rand said. "How is Georgia?"

"Not well," Maria said. "Whatever happened to her really stressed her out."

"What's going on?"

"Maybe it's better if she tells you herself."

Rand turned to Rachel. "Do you want to hang out here for a bit? I shouldn't be too long."

Rachel shrugged and joined the line to get a coffee. Rand and Libby went upstairs.

Harold the security guard was quite concerned as he

wrote out the visitors' nametags. "Apparently there was a huge commotion down the hall about an hour ago."

"Did you see anything?"

"Nothing," Harold said. "Not until Mr. and Mrs. Collins came back and found Miss Georgia on the floor."

In the hospital room, Georgia lay on her bed, covers pulled up to her chin and cannula running from her nostrils. Her father was seated by her side. She groaned when Rand entered.

"I should've known the ghost man would come." Then, she smiled at Libby. "Hey, Libby. Cool dress."

"Hey. Are you okay?" Libby took the desk chair to the side of the bed and sat down next to her.

Georgia looked awful. Her skin was whiter than usual and her eyes were red and puffy from crying. "I'm fine. Probably shouldn't have texted you, though." Her voice was thin and weak. "I should've known you'd bring your dad."

"I know you think he's a jerk right now, but he can help you," Libby said.

"He's already helped me enough."

"Come on, Georgia," Nick said. "Don't be like that. Tell Rand what happened so we can get to the bottom of this."

At the mere suggestion of reliving her tale, Georgia twisted in her bed and squeezed herself into a ball under the covers. Tears rimmed her eyes. Libby reached out and took her hand.

"Where did this picture come from?" Rand asked. "You did well in capturing it, but I need to know the whole context."

Georgia's breathing became shallow and labored, in

through the nose and out through the mouth, as if she were running on a treadmill instead of lying in bed.

"Georgia?" Maria said.

"Okay, okay." She coughed and then told them everything.

Rand's eyes moved around the room as he imagined Georgia's story. There were cracks in the wall and door right where Georgia said the exploding oxygen cylinders hit. The television that had been mounted the last time he visited was now on the floor, the screen broken.

"I took the picture after I saw him when the lights went out," Georgia finished.

"Honey, how could you see him if the lights weren't on?" Maria asked.

Georgia fixed her mother with a rigid stare, one that showed she refused to be disbelieved. "Because his body was darker than the dark around him."

Maria seemed confused, but Rand knew what she meant.

And he was very concerned. The girl had been attacked. However, he didn't want to use that word in front of the family right now and alarm them further.

Nick and Maria looked at him expectantly, as if he had the solution to all their problems.

"I'm sorry you went through this, Georgia," Rand began. "It seems Thomas's presence is stronger than he was letting on at the beginning. These spirits can do this as a way to protect themselves."

Rand had encountered spirits that knew what he was. Someone had once explained to him that it was in his aura. For that reason, spirits attempted to downplay their own energy so as to not be threatened by him.

Georgia rounded on him. "This wouldn't have happened if you hadn't pissed him off." She struggled to sit up in bed. Her mother tried to coax her, but she had none of it. When her back was against the headboard, she jabbed an accusing finger at him. "This is all your fault. He was fine before, but now he's mad. I told you to just leave him alone, and that he wasn't hurting anyone!"

"Georgia!" Nick scolded.

"I want you to leave. You being here is only going to make him angrier." Then she launched into a coughing fit.

Libby looked at him, frowning.

"I understand why you're frustrated," Rand said, "but you and I both know what happened here is not something Thomas would ever do to you. Something triggered this spirit and made it aggressive."

"*You* did!"

"It wasn't me. If he did this tonight, then he was always capable of doing it. That's what worries me."

"Then why did it take so long for this to happen?"

"Probably to get you to trust him. And it worked. Because now you're on his side and against me."

"Well, yeah," Georgia said. "Thomas was my friend. He was only sixteen when he died. Of course he's upset. But instead of being there for him, you come in and try to chase him away."

"Georgia," Nick said, "Rand only did what he did because he thought it was best for you. You heard him before. It isn't good or right for these... spirits to be here. They need to move on."

"I don't care," Georgia said. "All I know is he made everything worse."

"Georgia." Libby spoke for the first time, and everyone

looked at her. "Listen. I've grown up with this stuff my whole life. My dad's been dealing with it since before I was born. He's told me all about his past cases, and I've witnessed these things. Sometimes these pissed-off ghosts follow him home and try to take out their anger on him. Imagine being a little girl and having spirits attach themselves to your dad. I've seen so much crazy stuff, and I'm not even the Ghost Man. But he's right. These entities are so unpredictable that you can't have a normal life whenever they are around. You'll never be at peace. You'll always be on edge, waiting for the next thing to fall and break, or have your keys or purse go missing. Trust me, all of that's happened to me. So I know you're mad at my dad. He's easy to get mad at, and he pisses me off at least once a week. But believe me when I say he isn't here to upset you. He wants to do his best to help you. And he can. He's helped so many other people before."

Georgia fell silent as she retreated into herself. It slowly sunk in that she was fighting alone in her own corner. "Fine." The single word was weak, defeated.

Nick turned to Rand. "What do we do now? And this time... it needs to work." His eyes seemed to droop.

Rand already knew his next course of action before even arriving at the hospital. "I want to bring in a clairvoyant."

Everyone stared at him blankly. Everyone except Libby, who had met a few clairvoyants in her short life.

"What is that?"

"It's someone who is sensitive to the spiritual world. I can be sensitive, but there are others who are far more in tune than me. I work with them frequently. They are better able to communicate with spirits, sometimes acting as physical mediums, where the spirit can use the clair-voyant's voice."

Nick and Maria were even more confused.

"Sorry," Nick said. "I'm a little lost. But if you think it's best, I won't argue with you."

"I suggest this because this spirit obviously has more to say," Rand replied. "At first, all the evidence pointed to the fact that it was upset at having passed early. If that was all, then my cleansing in this room should have worked. But there are stronger emotions anchoring him here, and we need to find out what he wants so we are better able to send him on."

Libby nodded along.

"And um… when can we expect to meet this colleague of yours?"

Three knocks sounded at the door, and a nurse entered. "Sorry to break up the party, but visiting hours are over in ten minutes. Anyone not related to the patient needs to leave."

"Thanks, Donna," Nick said.

"I'll make calls first thing tomorrow and come back as soon as I can." To Rand, the case had become urgent. All his cases did when a restless, irritated ghost attacked someone.

And there was still the matter of Thomas's threat. It had been eleven days. Six days left. Rand still couldn't say if Georgia was destined to die from cystic fibrosis or an attack by Thomas. At that point, either seemed likely.

He forced himself to believe Thomas would be the cause. If not, then the girl would perish regardless of what he did for her. He kept that little detail to himself.

"And what do we do until then?" Nick asked.

"Cope. Be together. Keep an eye out for anything strange happening. If you see something, leave." Rand wished he had a better answer.

Nick didn't like the response, but he nodded anyway.

Rand and Libby returned to the Coffee Bean, where they found Rachel sitting alone at a table, playing on her phone with an empty cup in front of her. She looked up when she saw them approach. "How is everyone?"

"Not great," Rand said. "But I'm not out of ideas yet."

She frowned. "You seem stressed."

He shrugged.

"Mr. Rand."

He turned at the sound of his name. Harold the security guard had followed him down to the first floor.

"Harold," he said. "I didn't sign out. No one was at the desk when I went by, but I already threw my visitor sticker away."

Harold raised his hand. "Not a problem at all." He glimpsed at Rachel and scanned their matching formal attire. "Sorry to disturb. You folks seem busy."

"What can I do for you?"

"I was hoping you could look at something."

Rand glanced between Libby and Rachel. Both seemed tired, and it was already nearing midnight.

"It's about what's been going on with Miss Georgia."

"What about her?"

"Well, in the time since I last saw you, there's been some interesting things happening on the security footage. Given what you do, I was hoping you could take a look. I've shown every member of the team, but no one can make any sense of it."

"Paranormal activity?" Rand asked.

Harold winced. "I'd call it… unexplained."

"In Georgia's ward?"

"Not just there. All around the facility."

"And when did it start?"

"A few nights after you were last here."

After the cleansing, Rand thought.

He turned to Libby, who shrugged. "You should check that out, Dad."

Rand dug into his pockets and handed his keys to Rachel. "You two take my car. I'll grab a taxi."

"Is everything okay?" Rachel asked again.

"I have to look into this. I'll see you soon." He kissed her, and before she could protest too much he followed Harold down the corridor.

"I apologize for interrupting whatever you folks were up to," Harold said, "but I really do think you need to see this."

16

Harold led the way down several long hallways at the back of the hospital, then onto an elevator down to basement level 2. All the doors down there required badge access, which Harold had.

"I'm sure it goes without saying," Harold said. "But please keep this between you and me. The general public is not permitted in this area."

"Already figured."

They reached a double door with SECURITY plastered across.

"Wait here," Harold whispered, then went inside, leaving Rand alone in the silent hallway, grey and dim.

The door opened again and Harold motioned for him to enter.

Inside was another security guard, who watched the many monitors, all showing the live streams from the cameras throughout the hospital. The man looked Rand up and down.

"This is the ghost guy I told you about, Jerry," Harold said.

"Ah." Jerry popped his gum. "Glad you're here. Harold's all stressed out, so maybe you can tell him he's crazy."

Harold waved his hand dismissively at his coworker but smiled all the same.

They went into a smaller room on the other side of the main control panel, one filled with computers, metal shelves laden with boxes, and other equipment. A computer was set up on a workstation against the wall.

Harold shut the door behind them. "We can review the videos in here. Have a seat."

Rand lowered himself into the black plastic chair in front of the computer. Harold pushed the button on the monitor and it came back to life.

"A few days after you left, some other staff started going on about weird experiences in their own departments. One nurse even quit over it. I spent my lunch hours down here reviewing the film, and turns out I found a few things. I spliced them together for the next time you came by."

"Okay. Lay it on me."

Harold leaned his heavy frame over Rand's shoulder and used the mouse to click through some files saved in a separate folder.

The first video that Harold pulled up Rand recognized as the nurse station at the front of Georgia's ward. The image was grey-blue, soundless, with the time and date written on the bottom corner in white letters.

"You can follow Nica here," Harold said, pointing to

the nurse frozen in the frame. He clicked a button and the footage rolled.

Nica started at the nurse station, where she looked through papers and gathered them together. Then she set out down the hall, carrying her chart close to her chest. The camera angle switched over as soon as she walked out of frame. The colorful cartoon walls were greyed out by the footage's default lens.

"Watch this," Harold said.

The stream blurred. Static dotted the screen at the corners, but the camera continued recording. The picture was clear enough to see what happened next.

Nica's body jerked backward as if pulled by a strong force. She whirled around, startled. When she saw no one there, she clutched her chart against her chest and hurried the rest of the way down the hall.

"Did you catch that?" Harold asked.

"Yeah."

"It looked like something came up behind her and yanked her back."

"Does that static normally happen?"

"I noticed that too," Harold said. "And no, it doesn't. These cameras record in high quality."

That alarmed Rand. Spiritual activity had a tendency to interfere with electronic equipment. Since the glitches began right before Nica was grabbed, that was a bad sign.

"Is there more?"

"Oh boy." Harold shook his head and clicked a few times to load more footage. In the next video, it showed a normal square, carpeted room.

Rand noted the time at the bottom of the screen. Four o'clock in the morning.

"This is the playroom in one of the wards," Harold told him. "Obviously, none of the children are allowed in there at four, and there are no volunteers at that time."

"Right."

The seconds ticked away in the corner of the screen. The closet door opened by itself, painfully slow, as if blown by the slightest of breezes. Then it came to a halt, completely agape.

Static appeared again, causing the entire picture to blank out in zigzags of white and grey. When the video settled, the image had changed.

The contents of the closet had been thrown all over the floor. Game pieces were strewn about, play money covered the carpet like confetti, and the boxes that contained them were scattered. It was a huge mess. According to the time on the tape, it had only taken a few seconds for the closet to be ransacked.

And, of course, there was no perpetrator caught on video.

"When I came in that morning and I heard someone had thrown the board games all around, I checked the footage and this is what I found. They all thought it was one of the children, but there was no child on the tape. Even when it blanked out, no kid could have messed it up that fast and then gotten away *and* been lucky enough to do it right when the stream cut."

"Exactly," said Rand. "Did you bring this to the director's attention?"

Harold shrugged. "No. Even though the staff said it was one of the kids, they didn't want to point fingers. And besides, the video clearly shows it isn't the kids."

Rand agreed. He'd seen enough paranormal activity caught on security cameras to know.

"I even checked the door that day," Harold said. "It clicks in place when it's closed, so it's impossible for it to slip and open by itself. And if you were to open it just a fraction, then it stays put because the hinges are good."

"I believe you," Rand said.

The next piece of the stream showed Nica the nurse and one of the high school volunteers in the game room a few hours later, appraising the mess. They were talking, but none of the audio was captured.

After a lengthy discussion, the volunteer got down on her hands and knees and picked up the games, matching the pieces to the proper boards and sets and returning them to the closet.

"One more," Harold said. He clicked a few more buttons and brought up another tape.

They were back at the nurse station. The time was 3:58 in the morning on a different night. The seconds ticked by and no one was around.

"Nica does rounds every so often to make sure everyone is still in bed and that all is good," Harold said.

That must have been what she was doing. Then the same static happened again on the screen. It blurred and blanked out for three seconds. Rand watched the clock.

When it was clear, the nurse's station was a mess. Charts were on the ground. Papers had been thrown everywhere. Drawers were open and their contents— pens, paperclips, sticky notes—were all over the floor. Keyboards had been yanked from their computers and tossed away. Chairs that had been behind the desk were now on the far side of the room on their sides.

It would have taken time to create such a huge mess, yet it was all done within a few lost moments on the video.

The seconds ticked by, and eventually Nica walked back into the frame. She stopped short, looking around and scratching at her head. Then she ran away and was gone for several minutes before she returned with a security guard, who also looked confused.

"That's Keith," Harold said. "Works nights. He later told me he couldn't explain what happened, and that no one was there at all. Nica quit a few days later."

As the footage rolled on, it showed Nica and Keith picking up the nurse's station. It would take them the rest of the night, Rand knew.

Harold shut off the screen. "I'll keep monitoring. But I have a feeling it's only going to continue."

"It will," Rand said. "Thank you for showing this to me. This is exactly what I needed to see."

"What happens now? I'm worried for Miss Georgia."

"I am too. Now we deal with the problem. Don't worry, I have a plan."

"Is there any chance that this thing could... you know... hurt us?"

"Regardless, it's best if we remove this spirit as fast as possible."

Harold fixed him with a grim stare.

They returned to the main control room, where Jerry tapped at a game on his cell phone while the monitors streamed in front of him. It was the middle of the night, and there wasn't much activity going on.

"I trust everything has been thoroughly debunked," Jerry said without looking up.

"How I wish," said Harold.

Something on the video feed caught Rand's eye. Something that Jerry wasn't paying attention to. "Is this live?"

"Yeah." Jerry looked up for the first time. "Why?"

"Who's this?"

Rand pointed to the monitor in the corner. It showed the lobby of the hospital, now empty at the late hour. A teenage boy sat on one of the benches in the center of the room.

"It's a kid," Jerry said.

Rand checked his watch. "At midnight?"

"Maybe he's visiting?"

"No one else is in the lobby."

The three men watched the feed in silence. The boy did not move. Not to scratch an itch, not to look around, seemingly not even to breathe. He was like a statue.

"What's his deal?" Jerry said.

"Can you rewind this?" Rand asked. "To see how long he's been sitting there?"

"Yeah. Hang on." Jerry set his phone aside and clicked things on his control panel. He uploaded the feed to the screen right in front of him and rewound.

As the footage went backward, the time stamp in the corner reversed. An hour ticked away, then two hours. The boy had not moved.

"What the hell?" Jerry said. He mashed his finger down on the button and the rewinding sped up.

The time rolled back to five o'clock in the afternoon, where the frame filled with visitors and staff leaving for the day. They all walked past the boy, none acknowledging his presence. Four o'clock, three o'clock, two o'clock.

Then, somewhere between two and one, the boy disappeared within the space of a single frame. No footage of him coming or going.

Jerry looked up at Rand. "What did I just see?"

"Harold, did that kid look like Thomas?"

"Hard to make out on the camera, but yeah, there's definitely a resemblance." The man shook his head. "You have to help us, Rand."

Jerry busied himself rewinding and playing and analyzing the frames where Thomas disappeared, searching for any kind of rational explanation.

Rand knew he would not find one.

17

Rand's eyelids dropped closed as he drove, head bobbing up and down as if his body was trying to force a shutdown. It was one thirty in the afternoon and he'd tossed and turned the night before, thoughts consumed with Georgia. He was fueled only by three cups of coffee and a desperation to help the Collins family.

He pulled his orange Jeep into the parking lot of the elementary school. Children filled the playground, playing soccer or basketball—all form and rules disregarded. Their collective shrill voices carried to where his Jeep idled.

The teachers on duty stood in a huddle near the fence —three women and one man. The man spotted him, said something to the group, and the others turned around. They knew Rand's car. He was the only person in town who owned a bright orange Jeep.

Rand picked out Katie among the teachers. Her eyes lingered on him the longest.

Katie's colleagues murmured to each other for a long time, casting sideways glances at him. Eventually, Katie broke away from the group and went through the gate in the chain-link fence that separated the playground from the parking lot.

She sauntered toward him, arms folded across her body, looking down at the pavement.

Rand rolled down the passenger window.

"What are you doing?" she whispered through clenched teeth. "You can't just show up at my workplace. Especially an elementary school. That's creepy."

"Everyone over there knows who I am," Rand said. "And that I'm not a predator."

"Maybe not a predator towards kids, but you're definitely a predator to me." Her voice was icy.

"That's a colder reception than I anticipated, I'll admit," Rand said. "But you know I wouldn't come unless it was important. I need to talk to you."

"About what?" she shot back. "What could there *possibly* be left for you and me to talk about?"

"Business," he answered. "And business only. I'm hoping you're able to let the personal stuff slide for now."

"I can't let the personal stuff slide, Rand. And our business is resolved."

"Again, I told you I wouldn't come unless I needed to, and I'm desperate. This isn't about me. Can you sit?" He nodded toward the passenger seat.

"Your window is down, I can hear you just fine."

"It would be better if you sat."

Katie rolled her eyes, then opened the door and got into the car. The other teachers on duty watched them with unbroken gazes. None of the kids were paying them any attention at all.

"What's this about?" Katie asked. She pushed up the sleeve of her purple sweater and checked her watch. "Recess ends in six minutes. You have three."

"I'm involved in a case," Rand said.

"You're always involved in a case."

"I need you for this one."

Katie groaned. "Don't tell me that."

"Please. You're the best there is."

"I'm the only one there is."

That was true. Katie held kind of a monopoly on the clairvoyant market in town.

"You know I wouldn't call you if it wasn't serious. It's about a little girl. She's fifteen years old."

"I spend my day with ten-year-olds."

"This one is sick. Very sick. Terminal, actually."

Katie finally looked at him earnestly for the first time. "What do you mean?"

"Over at St. Mary's. Her parents came to me after class, told me their daughter speaks to the ghost of a friend who passed away three months back. They weren't sure if it was real or just her way of dealing with her situation, so they wanted me to get to the bottom of it. Got some EVP of her talking to the ghost, and it told her the day of her death."

"Oh my God," Katie said, her eyes growing wide. Like him, she knew the gravity of asking a spirit about the hour of death. "That's so terrible."

"Here's how it's complicated. Her disease is terminal, and she could pass away at any time. So I don't know if the spirit was talking about her illness or if he was going to do something to directly cause her death."

"So it could be that no matter what you do, you still lose her," Katie said.

"Exactly." Rand sighed. That little detail hadn't failed to gnaw at him in the back of his mind. "Anyway, I did a cleansing in the room and sent the ghost away. Figured I knew the spirit's story—the kid passed too early and he was hanging around, so I didn't bother to call in a clairvoyant. But then, last night, the ghost came back and was upset. It attacked her in her hospital room. Held the doors closed and blew out her oxygen tanks. It's not even isolated to her room anymore, either. It's causing disruption in other areas of the hospital, too. I've seen the security footage."

"And?" Katie asked, suddenly interested.

"The usual. It's throwing stuff around in the middle of the night, knocking things over, making a big mess. You know, just trying to get attention. People notice it now, and if we don't do something about it, then it'll only get crazier."

Katie let out a deep breath and settled in the seat. Her teacher colleagues murmured amongst each other, probably speculating on why Katie was talking so long to an ex-boyfriend—one they had no doubt heard so much about.

"I need to bring you in," Rand said. "I want you to talk to him, find out exactly what he wants, because it seems I misjudged his desires. You can smooth-talk him into the afterlife, send him away, save this family loads of grief in this already difficult time for them, and then, after that...

we can never see each other again if that's what you want."

"Of course that's what I want," Katie shot back.

There was no code of conduct in the ghost-hunting business, but if Rand were to ever write one, he would mandate one never sleep with their clairvoyant.

Something about dealing with the supernatural had brought them closer over the years, and they had ended up in a relationship. Since they had worked together so often, that had inevitably ended up in disaster.

"I can't involve myself with this stuff again," Katie said. "Or with you. I have a normal life now. A normal job." She gestured toward the playground. "I love my students and I love what I do. I don't want all that… chaos."

It was true. For many long years, Katie had used her special gift for good. But over time, Rand had seen the all-nighters and the stressful, terrifying situations take their toll on her. She was young, only twenty-seven if he remembered correctly, but she already looked about five years older.

"I understand," Rand told her. "I'm not asking you to go back to it completely. I'm only asking you for just this once. For the little girl. If it were any other client, I wouldn't ask. But you wouldn't believe how cool Georgia is. And how much her family has already been tormented."

Katie took in a long, heavy breath and let it out slowly. "Rand. You know how it is. There can never be just one—this is a lifestyle. And it's not even one that I can choose. I was lucky to get out of it when I did, and if I go back, I'll be roped in forever. My life is good now. It's normal."

"You're denying your gift," Rand said. "You were given

it for a reason. And I'll make sure that this is the last case you ever get involved in, at least from me. If you do this, I promise, you'll never hear from me again." He held out his hand.

Katie looked at it, considering. Rand knew it wasn't him personally that was the main problem. It was the life of chasing ghosts and dealing with the spiritual world.

Movement on the other side of Katie caught Rand's eye. A boy was chasing a rolling basketball through the parking lot. He ran up to it and bent down to snatch it up.

"One of your kids got loose," Rand said.

Katie followed his gaze.

The kid had run between the Jeep and the other teachers' line of sight. Yet none of them reacted.

Rand's mouth went dry.

The boy straightened, basketball underneath his arm and pressed against his side. Now that Rand had a better view, he looked more like a teenager than an elementary school child.

And he looked Rand directly in the eyes. Although the midday sun was bright, and he wasn't that far away, a shadow still fell over his face, obscuring it.

Katie looked back at him. "What kid?"

"Shit," Rand muttered. He threw open the Jeep door and ran around the front. But in the split second he'd taken his eyes off the boy, the kid had vanished. He checked between the parked cars nearby, but he wasn't there.

"Rand, what are you doing?" Katie shouted through the passenger window.

He returned to the Jeep and shut the door behind him.

Katie looked at him, worried, but he knew she understood what was going on. "How long?" she asked.

"First time I've seen him."

She swallowed. "So he's appearing to you now."

"I told you it's escalated."

Often, once the spirits realized what he was and that he was against them, they'd switch their efforts to him. Try to scare him off the case. Since that never worked, their attacks eventually turned physical in time.

"At least I know you're not making it all up," Katie said, then sighed. "I'll go with you just this once since you're starting to see apparitions. And when we go, you will not tell anyone about this. And then when it's over, you are not to contact me about any case ever again."

"Deal," Rand said.

"I live with my boyfriend now," Katie said. "You can pick me up from his house. He'll be out of town for business, so he won't know I'm gone."

Funny. He hadn't heard about her getting a new boyfriend. "Sure."

"I'll text you the location. Is your number still the same?"

"Yes."

"A miracle with all the phones you go through."

Spirits liked to smash his stuff when they got mad at him. That was why he couldn't have nice things.

She got out of the car as the bell rang and the children lined up. She rejoined the other teachers, all waiting expectantly for her to tell them why in the world her ex-boyfriend had shown up to her work, but Rand noticed that she didn't indulge their curiosity.

Rand started the engine and drove away, scanning the parking lot one more time for the boy and his basketball.

18

That night, Rand wolfed down the dinner he had prepared for him and Rachel. Chicken thighs and rice. It was one of the few recipes he'd perfected.

"So, let me get this straight," Rachel said, taking another sip of wine. "You have to go back to the hospital tonight?"

"Yes."

"And do a second little ritual thing? This time with a… what?"

"A clairvoyant. She's more sensitive to the spiritual world than most normal people. It's also easier for her to communicate with presences. After we figure out what this ghost wants, then we'll be better able to successfully send it on its way."

"And how do you know this clairvoyant?"

"We used to date."

Rachel choked on her wine, then wiped her mouth with the back of her hand. "Sorry?"

"Well, really we only hooked up. But we hooked up a lot, so does that count as dating? Maybe just a relationship. We had a relationship, yeah, but we never actually went on any dates. If that makes sense."

"You're seeing an ex tonight?"

"Yes, but not like that. She's going for Georgia." He took another mouthful of food.

"I'm… not sure how I feel about that."

"It will be weird for me too. Before, it was like hooking up with someone from work, because we used to team up on a lot of cases a long time ago. But for Georgia Collins, I had to pull her in. She's the most gifted of anyone I've ever met, and the family needs her. That's all it is."

Rand wasn't stupid. He could see that Rachel didn't like that he was seeing an ex-girlfriend, and he knew his casual explanations weren't doing much to assuage her feelings. But the case came first, always. And he didn't like to lie to the people he cared about, so he gave her the blunt truth. If she was uncomfortable with that, there wasn't much he could do. It was the nature of the job.

He finished his food and dropped his plate in the sink. Rachel's food remained half-eaten in front of her.

"I'll be home late," Rand said, kissing her forehead. He threw his keys in his jacket pocket and picked up his bag, already packed with the things he'd need for the night. "This will be the last time I have to go there. I'm sure we can take care of this spirit tonight."

"Yeah," Rachel said, swirling her wine around in the glass.

Just then, thunder boomed in the sky. The clouds opened up, and rain came hurtling down.

Rand frowned. "Great."

"Drive carefully," Rachel said, her voice still flat and unimpressed.

———

As he drove, Rand tapped the latest text from Katie. She'd dropped a pin—the location of her boyfriend's house. He hadn't looked at it closely when she'd sent it, but now he squinted at the map, his eyes darting between the road and his phone.

The pin was in a very nice part of the town, where the houses were massive and the families were rich.

That couldn't be right. Could it?

Sure enough, Rand followed the pin right to Azalea Lakes, the most prestigious neighborhood in the city, filled with small mansions, huge yards, and three-car garages. Rand had never been inside but had seen plenty of pictures on the internet.

The security guard stopped him at the booth.

"Name?" the man asked, clearly bored. The rain still pelted down, falling into Rand's rolled-down window.

"Randolph Casey."

The man typed on his computer. "Rand Casey?"

"Yeah. Sure."

"Here to see Mr. Albright?"

That must be the boyfriend. "Katie, actually."

"Ah yes, also the residence of Katie Fitz." The security guard cast him a suspicious, sidelong glance. "Does Mr. Albright know you're here to visit his home?"

"I'm sure he has full access to your records of who comes and goes," Rand said, meeting the guard's gaze.

"You're right. He does. Have a good evening, Mr. Casey." His voice was ice cold.

The gate opened and Rand proceeded through, knowing that Mr. Albright would surely hear about his little visit. He hoped it wouldn't cause any trouble for Katie.

Rand pulled up in front of the house and stared at it for a long while. It was huge. He could only chuckle and shake his head. All his ex-women had a habit of spring-boarding from him to rich, stable, successful men. Men who didn't spend their time chasing ghosts around dark rooms.

The front door opened and Katie emerged, pulling her jacket hood over her head as she ran across the yard toward his Jeep—no short distance. He reached over and opened the door for her, and she climbed in. Despite the coat, she was still soaked. The rain fell thick and accumulated into giant puddles on the sides of the road, unable to drain quickly enough.

"Let's get this over with," Katie said.

"I hear you." He turned around and pulled away from the house. The security guard opened the gate for them on the way out and let them proceed without any questions, but he glowered at Rand. Katie, however, gave him a friendly wave, which he woodenly returned.

"That guy thinks I'm here to cause trouble for Mr. Albright," Rand said.

"He likes Mitch a lot."

"Mitch, huh? And when did you meet Mitch? What's Mitch do?"

"Rand…"

Rand shut up. None of that mattered, anyway. Only Georgia Collins.

19

Rand found Harold waiting for him at the Coffee Bean, just as the man had said. An almost empty cup of black brew rested in front of him while he stared blankly at the table, wringing his hands together.

"Evening," Rand said, and Harold snapped out of his trance. "This is my colleague, Katie. She'll be assisting me."

Harold forced a smile and stood to shake Katie's hand.

"You all right?" Rand asked.

"Just nervous."

"I am too," Rand said, not untruthfully. His wet jacket froze to him in the chilly hospital air. "Has everything been arranged?"

"I've talked to the nurses working tonight. They've agreed to give you folks two hours alone time on the ward. This took a lot of convincing; you're lucky that Donna's the shift lead, and that she's had her own weird experiences up there lately."

"Understood," Rand said.

"All these ladies could lose their jobs for abandoning their posts," Harold said. It was the most serious Rand had ever seen him. "Me as well for being part of it. I know you won't, but they've asked me to remind you not to take advantage of all this."

"You have my word," Rand said. A heaviness settled on him, pressing against his heart at asking the man to put his own job on the line for them.

Harold nodded once and took out his cell—a plain flip phone that must have been ten years old. He punched in the numbers, eyes squinting as he struggled to read the tiny keypad. "They're here," was all he said into the receiver before closing the phone. "Donna and the others will vacate. I'll walk you up, then make myself scarce."

"Got it."

Harold offered him a walkie-talkie. "Borrowed this from Jerry. If you need to get in touch with me, I'll be on the other end. Channel nine is never used by the staff, so tune in to that one."

Rand took it and twisted the knob. It flared to life with a burst of static. He clipped the device to his belt. "Anything else?"

"Kick this bastard out of my ward. I'm tired of seeing so many good people go through so much."

The three started toward the elevator. Once inside, Harold pressed the button for the tenth floor.

"Where will you be?" Rand asked.

"I'll head to security and keep an eye on everything from the cameras. Jerry's off tonight and Juan called in sick, so it'll just be me. If anything—"

A tight hand clutched Rand's arm. He turned in time

to see Katie stumble backward and fall hard against the elevator's back wall.

"Oh," Rand said, rushing to support her. She leaned heavily against him. "Katie, what's wrong?"

Her palm went to her chest, which heaved with deep breaths. "I can't," she managed between gasps.

"Katie, what is it?"

"I'll get help," Harold said, reaching for his radio.

"No!" Rand held out his hand, and Harold froze, confused and nervous.

"Katie. What do you feel?"

"It's so powerful," she said. Sweat had broken out on her forehead and her eyes welled with tears. "So much."

The elevator chimed at each floor as it rose.

Ding. 6.

Ding. 7.

"I can't go up there," she said.

"You have to," Rand said.

"I've never felt anything so—"

Ding. 8.

Katie's knees gave way, and she slumped to the floor. "Stop the elevator! It's getting worse!"

Harold reached for the emergency button.

"No, Harold!"

The man looked between him and Katie, unsure of what to do.

"Rand," Katie said. "It's too much. There's something big up there. We need to leave."

Ding. 9.

Rand put both his hands on Katie's cheeks, ice cold and slick with sweat and looked into her eyes. "We've never run away before, Katie. It's just not what we do. We have to be strong for the people who can't be. Remember?"

She slowly nodded between his palms. The tears broke and began to stream down her cheeks.

Ding. 10.

The doors slid open.

Harold pressed a button on the panel that froze the elevator in place. As he'd promised, the ward was empty. It was after hours, so half the lights had been turned off, leaving the corridor in a dim light, the shadows edging the colorful cartoon animals and children on the walls. The nurse station was vacant.

"Can you stand?" Rand said. His words were loud against the silent ward in front of them.

Katie sniffed and nodded curtly. She crawled to the other side of the elevator and used the sides to support herself. Once she was steady, she stepped out into the ward.

She froze, then looked around. Brought her hands to her mouth to keep herself from crying out.

Be strong, Rand thought. He had never seen her react so intensely before. Nor had he known her to get visions so fast. *We weren't even there yet.*

Katie walked toward the large area near the nurse station, focusing all around her as if a crowd of distracting people surrounded her.

"What's going on?" Harold whispered.

"She senses something," Rand whispered back. "She can feel what's there. Things that we can't see."

Katie's shoulders shook as she sobbed, but still, she pressed on. She crossed her arms, rubbing her hands up and down her sleeves as if they were crawling with bugs.

"What is this?" she whispered to herself. "How can this be?"

"Should we do something?" Harold asked. "She seems upset."

"Leave her be for now. Let her work."

Katie leapt to the side, appearing to be startled by something to her right. But Rand saw nothing. "I'm sorry," she said through her tears. "I don't know what to do for you. I can't—"

She was speaking to someone. *Does she already hear voices? That's unusual without first going into a trance.*

"Please. It isn't my fault," Katie said.

Rand noted she was looking toward the ground rather than to the corners of the room, where she normally focused. Spirits had a penchant for lingering in the corners.

"Rand, this can't go on," Harold said, no longer whispering. "If you don't do something, I will."

"Please! No!" Katie screamed, then turned and ran. She bounded toward the stairwell, where she banged open the door and disappeared.

"Katie!" Rand called, following her.

Katie's footsteps clanged and echoed off the grey walls of the narrow staircase as she ran down.

"Katie!" Rand's voice boomed around him. Over the railing, her figure sprinted down, winding in a circle along the steps that hugged the wall, like water down a bathtub drain.

"I have to get out of here!" Katie shouted back at him.

"Wait for me!"

Finally, he caught up to her. She sat on the last step by

the door that led to level six, her back to him, leaning against the metal handrail and crying.

Rand dropped down next to her and she put her head on his shoulder. He gave her time to get it all out, wondering what on earth she could have possibly seen.

"What's going on?" he whispered to her.

"Rand, we can't stay here."

"You know that's impossible." He kept his tone gentle. "What was it? Was it Thomas?"

Katie looked up at him, eyes wide and red and full of tears. "Rand. The spirits of children on the tenth ward... there are *hundreds* of them."

20

undreds.

It took Rand a minute to process what he'd heard. "What?"

Katie wiped her eyes and sat up straight. The anxiety brought on by being on the tenth floor subsided. "There are hundreds of spirits up there. They rushed me all at once. They grabbed at me, cried at me, begged me to look at them. I couldn't hear any voices, but I saw it all on their little faces."

Rand swallowed. "How is that possible?"

No wonder his cleansing ceremony hadn't been effective. Could it be that Georgia was interacting with more than one spirit?

"Surely lots of children have passed on that ward over the years," Katie went on. "Some I could sense have been there for decades. There were *so many*."

"I don't get it," Rand said. "How is it that hundreds of kids could not move on?"

Katie let out her shaky breath, steadying herself. "All of

them had harmless energy. They're innocent. But there was one not like the rest."

"One?"

"I didn't see him. But I felt him stronger than all the others. One of them is dark and angry." She looked at him. "And he did not want us there."

Rand licked his lips. "They're trapped," he said. "Whoever this one is, it's keeping the rest from moving on."

"I think so," Katie said, sniffing again. "I could sense that all the kids wanted to do was leave, but they couldn't. They were so desperate and it broke my heart. I'll never be able to unsee that ever again."

Rand clenched his jaw. He never would have insisted Katie join him had he known what they were truly up against. As usual, everyone around him was affected by his cases and his life.

"How do you feel?" Rand asked her.

"A bit better."

"Do you need to go?"

She paused to consider before she answered. "No. I'm here, so we should finish. There's a huge problem on that ward, so I can't in good conscience leave those children there now."

"I'm sorry. I had no idea they were there."

"You couldn't have known. What do we do now?"

"You said there's the one that doesn't feel like the others?"

"Yes. It's very different from the rest," Katie said.

"That's who we need to get in contact with."

HAROLD WAS WAITING for them at the top of the stairs. "Everything all right, folks?"

"Yes," Katie said. "I was just caught off guard with what I found up here. It's been a while since the last time I've done this."

Rand nodded at her little white lie. Despite the rough beginning, Katie would pull through with the strength and determination he'd always known her to have.

Harold, though, seemed skeptical. "You guys sure?"

"Yes," Rand said. "Now it's time to get to work." He checked his watch. They had about an hour and forty minutes left before the nurses returned to their post.

"What do you need me to do?" Harold asked.

"Head to security. We'll take the rest from here." By Rand's side, Katie's eyes darted around the room, likely taking in all the spirits that had desperately hoped to see her return.

"Remember the radio. I'm only a call away."

"Same."

Rand knocked on Georgia's door and Nick answered. He stood aside and let them in.

"Everything all right?" he asked, checking his watch.

"Sorry to be late. This is my colleague, Katie. Katie, this is Nick and Maria and their daughter Georgia." Georgia sat on the bed, hands pressed underneath her thighs. She seemed uneasy.

"Nice to meet you all." Katie had composed herself well, hiding the fact that she had recently been crying.

"This is the… what do you call it?" Nick asked.

"Clairvoyant," Katie answered. "Yes, that's me."

"And you can help?"

"I am confident that I can."

Nick sighed in relief. "Good. We're out of ideas here."

"What about you?" Rand asked Georgia. "How have you been since last night?" She only shrugged. "Anything paranormal going on?"

"Not so far," she said. "But I'm sure now that you're here something else of mine will get smashed." Her television had not been replaced. "If you're the ghost man, I guess that makes her the ghost lady."

Katie smirked. "I can get on board with that nickname."

"Do you piss off ghosts like he does? Because if you do, then maybe we should rethink this. He's already angry enough."

"We're not here to make any ghosts angry," Katie said, taking a step closer. "We are here to clear this place so they will leave you in peace."

"Right, right, I've heard it all before. Can we just get it over with so I can go to bed?"

"What do we need to do?" Maria asked. "Anything?"

"We'll try to communicate with the spirit," Rand said. "For that, Katie will act as a medium and allow the entity to reach us through her voice. She's done it many times before and is quite the expert, so there should be nothing to worry about."

Rand hoped that was true. *There is one not like the rest.*

"Like the movies?" Georgia said.

"In a way," Katie said. "But mediums have existed for hundreds of years before they started appearing in movies."

"I think it would be best to have the room as empty as possible," Rand said. "So, Nick and Maria, are you able to let us have some private time? Maybe head down to the Coffee Bean?"

Nick and Maria were clearly uncomfortable with the idea but were pliable enough. "What about Georgia?" Maria asked.

"She should stay," Rand said. "Since she's been the target, it will be easier to attract the spirit and convince him to open up."

"Like bait?" Nick asked.

"Not bait," Rand said. "More like a familiar face."

"Nothing will happen to her," Katie said. "We promise. The only contact will come through me."

The couple looked at each other for a long time before silently coming to an agreement.

"On the bright side," Georgia said, "if I like this, then maybe I've found what I want to be when I grow up. A medial."

"A *medium*. And please try to be more serious about this," Maria said, kissing her daughter on the forehead. "We'll be downstairs. Call if you need us."

Then they were gone.

"Had I known I was coming face-to-face with a ghost tonight," Georgia said, glancing in the mirror and smoothing her hair, "I would have put on eyeliner."

"We want them to leave, remember?" Rand said.

"Them?"

"Him," Rand said quickly.

He got to work on preparations, first by taking Georgia's desk chair and two extras from her closet, then setting them up near each other in a triangle. On the floor between them, he placed a glass of water, a plate of bread, and three candles from his bag, then lit them. Incense went on Georgia's desk and her nightstand. The sweet, powerful smell quickly filled the small room. Rand opened the door just a crack—open doors were much more inviting to spirits.

Georgia was quite interested in the setup. "Is he supposed to be like a stray? Feed him and he'll come."

"It's best to have offerings ready when contacting the other side," Rand remarked.

"Thomas liked the ice cream from downstairs. But that'll be closed now."

"We don't have to be precise."

"Good. Because that would melt."

"Do you have a picture of Thomas?"

Georgia surveyed the mounted corkboard near her bed and removed the pin from a photo among the dozens already there. It was the first time Rand had ever actually seen Thomas. It was a selfie of him and Georgia, him a few inches taller with wavy dark hair swooped to the side, matching cannulas falling from their nostrils. Rand propped the picture against the glass of water.

With the preparations made, Rand turned off the lights and instructed them to sit in the chairs, Katie at the head.

"Everyone hold hands," she said. When they did, the trio formed a circle around the candles and offerings. The room was dark, and the only light flickered from the tiny flames in front of them. "Remember, what we're about to do is simple and has been done for centuries, but it will only work if we keep our minds open to what we may find. Whatever happens, listen to me, and do not break the circle until I tell you to." She spoke strongly, as she always did when instructing newcomers to her séance.

But, even in the flickering candlelight, he could see the fear behind her eyes. "Let's begin."

Rand felt Georgia's hand tighten on his own.

"Beloved Thomas, we bring you gifts from life into death. Be guided by the light of this world and visit upon us."

Georgia looked around the room. But the whole place was just as silent as before.

"Beloved Thomas, we bring you gifts from life into death. Be guided by the light of this world and visit upon us."

Katie's palm in Rand's was clammy and her breathing was nervous and uneven. After a prolonged silence, Rand asked, "What do you see?"

"We're not alone," Katie whispered.

Georgia's head darted left and right, up and down, for the first time uneasy.

"Who is here?" Rand asked.

"So many of them."

The candle flames bent and danced all in the same direction as if blown by a light wind.

"I know that you all are here," Katie said, voice trembling, "but please, give us a sign anyway."

The place erupted in clamor. Rapping and beatings on all the walls and floor surrounding them, like hundreds of hands banging every inch of the surfaces that made up the room.

Georgia gasped and jerked in her chair. Rand clenched her hand, afraid she might try to break the circle.

The noises ceased.

"We welcome you here," Katie said. "But there is one among you called Thomas. We wish to speak to him."

Katie had a sharp intake of breath as if someone had pressed cold hands against her skin.

"What now?" Rand asked.

Katie didn't answer. Again the flames flickered, this time so much that they were almost extinguished. But after whatever movement had caused them to shift ceased, the fire regrew.

"What is it?" Rand asked again.

"They've all gone."

Rand straightened. That was new to him. Usually, you had to struggle to bring spirits to a séance, then had to struggle again to make them leave. "Gone?"

"They fled as soon as I mentioned the name."

"I don't get it," Georgia said. "There's more than one ghost?"

"Let's call them back," Rand said.

Katie shook her head. "They won't come. Not as long as we ask for that specific name." Katie licked her lips. "There is one left lingering, though. She's by the door." Her voice was a soft whisper, as if afraid she would frighten the spirit away.

Rand glanced toward the door, but he saw no one there.

"Can you help us?" Katie asked. "Can you bring us the one called Thomas?"

Katie watched the door, and Rand watched Katie. Long moments passed as she waited for a response. Finally, Katie deflated. "She ran away too."

"Call out for him directly, then."

Katie fixed him with a hard look. "I have a bad feeling about that."

"This is who we need to speak to."

Katie took a deep breath. "We wish to speak to the one called Thomas. If you are here, please make yourself known."

Nothing.

"Thomas, please join us here. We have come to speak with you. We want to know what troubles you so we can help you. Do not be afraid."

They waited for a long while. Rand found his heart went from beating to pounding, and while he hadn't been involved in a séance in a while, it was far from his first. *Why am I getting uneasy?*

"He's coming," Katie whispered, clenching his hand. "He's in the hall now."

Her eyes traced the wall over Rand's shoulder. On the other side of that wall was the outside corridor. Katie's gaze drifted along it as if she could see through the wall. Then rested on the door. "He's here." Her voice was thin and terse.

"What do you see?"

"I can't see him. But I can feel him. And it's not good."

Rand glanced at Georgia, who looked frightened and full of questions.

"T-Thomas. I sense you are here. But please, give us a sign."

There was a single, huge rap from the ceiling as if all the pipes and fixtures were about to burst through the plaster and crash to the floor.

She hesitated before continuing. "Thank you for coming. We're here to help you. Tell us what you need us to know."

Katie let the silence linger on. Raw nerves clawed at the inside of Rand's stomach; he could not remember the last time he'd been anxious in the presence of a spirit.

Katie only frowned. "Thomas, there must be something we can talk about."

Her eyes were still at the door, and she looked upset.

After another long pause, Rand asked, "What's going on? Is he talking?"

"He refuses to say anything," she said.

"He's silent?"

"No." For the first time since Thomas had arrived, she took her eyes from the door. Even in the dim candlelight, Rand saw that her tears had returned. "He's speaking. But refuses to answer my questions. He says there is only one person here he will deal with, and it's you."

Usually, the spirits were happy enough to communicate through Katie. But Thomas had been stubborn up until then. Perhaps it was because Thomas was already familiar with Rand from the last cleansing ceremony.

Or angry at Rand for trying to get rid of him, more likely.

"Okay. We can do that. I'm listening."

"No," Katie said. "He's only got one message for you. He keeps saying 'follow me.'"

21

A new wave of dread crashed into Rand.

"Follow him?"

"He's not saying anything else," Katie said. "And he won't leave until you do."

"Don't do it," Georgia whispered. She looked utterly terrified. "Or let me at least come with you."

Katie shook her head. "He wants Rand alone."

"Right," Rand said, pushing away any fear that may have crept in. Thomas would be able to sense it, so he had to remove it. "No problem. I'll follow him."

This means he has something to show me, Rand thought.

"First, though, we need to end the séance properly," Rand said.

To the room, Katie said, "Spirits, thank you for coming. You can return to your own world." Then to Rand and Georgia, she said, "We'll let our hands go on the count of three. One. Two. Three."

They broke the circle all at the same time. Katie blew out the candles.

As soon as she did, the door creaked open by itself, all the way.

"Guess I'll get going," Rand said, standing from the chair.

"Call if you need us," Katie said, and for the first time in a long while, looked concerned about his wellbeing.

The lights flickered in the corridor outside. The hallway was long and straight, the nurse station at the end abandoned. It looked like the power had gone out and only the backup lights were on, but even those blinked off occasionally, plunging Rand into complete darkness as he stalked down the tiled floor. It was like he'd stepped into a new dimension.

Something knocked on the wall, once just near him, again farther down, and then a third time at the end of the hallway, which echoed back to him.

He followed the sounds, moving cautiously, trying to look everywhere at once. The smiling and innocent cartoon characters on the walls looked a lot more menacing in the blinking light like a twisted audience watching him walk toward a terrible fate.

Often, instead of speaking, spirits wanted him to follow them. They were known to lead him to any possibility of things—sometimes the site of the tragedy that kept them bound to earth, and other times it was the location of their unmarked grave no one had ever discovered.

So when a spirit beckoned Rand to follow, he knew he had to.

The radio on his belt came to life with static. "Rand, everything all right?" Harold asked.

Rand had forgotten about it already. He unclipped it

and brought it to his mouth and pressed the button. "Yeah. All good."

"I've got you on camera in the corridor by yourself. What's going on?"

Rand was glad to have eyes on him for this. "Playing a little round of follow the ghost."

No response for a few seconds. "Your time's almost up. Hurry and do what you need to do."

Halfway down the hall, Rand heard the unmistakable sound of bare feet pattering on the tile floor behind him. Running straight for him.

He whirled around just as they came close, only to find no one there. Then, laughter from the other direction where he'd been walking before. When he turned back, again there was nothing.

So we're going to play games.

He reached into his pocket and withdrew the same small recording device he'd planted in Georgia's room and pressed the button to record.

Rand approached the beginning of the corridor, where it opened into the round nurse station area. The circular desk created a cubicle filled with computers, charts, and papers. The only sound was a telemetry machine that beeped as the lines of the heart rhythm dipped up and down, remotely monitoring a patient somewhere else on the ward.

Rand shivered as the temperature suddenly plunged to freezing as if he'd walked into a meat locker. His damp clothes clung to him, jabbing tiny, invisible icicles into his skin.

"I know you're here, Thomas," Rand said to the empty

room. "Show yourself." He tightened his grip on the recorder in his hand.

Something moved in his peripheral. He turned just in time to see a young boy duck below the counter on the other side of the nurse station, out of view. Rand rushed around the circular desk, but when he got there the boy had vanished.

"Enough playing around, Thomas," Rand said.

Beep. Beep. Beep.

The telemetry machine picked up its pace, the heart rate increasing, the beats per minute shooting up impossibly fast.

Beep-beep-beep-beep

Then the machine shut off and the screen went black. The room was silent now.

Rand brought the radio to his mouth and pressed the button. "Harold, are you still watching?"

"I'm here. What's up?"

"Are you seeing anything on your cameras?"

"Nothing besides you running around like a crazy guy."

"There's an apparition. He's messing with me. Wants me to follow him."

A rack of charts tipped off the desk and crashed to the ground, sending papers everywhere.

"That's enough, Thomas," Rand said. "Just talk to me without being destructive. You have my attention."

"Holy moly," Harold breathed into the radio. "I saw that."

The door to the stairwell that Katie ran into earlier opened. He turned in time to catch a small figure disappear through it before it fell back into place.

"The door just opened and closed by itself," Harold said.

"Looks like I'm heading for the stairs."

Rand followed the apparition to the stairwell. He stood in place for a few minutes, waiting for further instruction.

Up or down?

Someone fell from above like they had leapt from the upper story, their body disappearing in a flash past Rand's line of sight and startling him, causing him to jump back.

Rand rushed to the rail and looked down, but the jumper had vanished.

Down.

No matter how softly he stepped, his footsteps clanged and echoed through the narrow room. Round and round, down the stairs, on edge, waiting for the next sudden appearance of the apparition. He kept a tight grip on the cold handrail. Rand had encountered a spirit or two that enjoyed sending hapless victims tumbling down steps—falling victim to it more than once.

The radio gave a sharp burst of feedback.

When Rand came around to the sixth floor, the sign unhooked and fell, turning into a nine. He paused. It swung back and forth on its remaining screw, squeaking until it came to a halt.

"Why'd you stop?" Harold asked.

"He wants me on six."

There was silence for a moment, and then Harold came back in a burst of static. "That's out of bounds."

"I never assumed he'd take me to a public area."

"You don't have badge access."

As soon as he said it, the door creaked open by itself.

"Thomas does. Can you check if I'm clear?"

"Hold on."

Harold disappeared for a few minutes. As Rand waited, he stared at the door, waiting for something else to happen. The room on the other side appeared abnormally dark for a hospital ward.

"No one's around," Harold said. "Place is usually quiet after hours. But here's the thing: the power's out."

"Power's out?"

"Yeah. Sixth floor is on generator power. Same as the tenth. But wards seven through nine are fine."

"That's not the storm, then." *Only the places where Thomas has been are affected.*

"Just be careful, Rand."

Rand opened the door all the way and went into the sixth-floor corridor. As Harold had said, the hallway was dark, only lit by the scant backup lights.

A second later, the door to the stairwell slammed shut behind him. Rand pressed against it, but it didn't budge. Locked. Or something was holding it closed from the other side.

"You should be able to open it from that side," Harold said.

"It's stuck."

"Wait a minute. I can give you remote clearance from here. Okay, try now."

It still would not budge. "Don't worry about it. That way is going backward."

"Yeah, but I'd like to know you have a path out of there if you need it."

"We're moving forward. What's on this floor that I—"

When Rand turned, there was someone on the far end of the corridor. With the backup lights, it only appeared as a black figure. A child's silhouette, his hand gripping an IV pole.

Rand froze. It was the longest the apparition had appeared to him, and it had changed form. Now it presented itself as a patient.

"Rand?" Harold said.

"Are you seeing this?"

"Seeing what?"

"He's staring right at me."

"I don't see anything. But..."

"But what?"

"The video feed is distorting. I might lose you."

The presence is stronger now.

"Thomas," Rand called down the hall. His clear voice echoed all the way. The dark figure did not react to the name. Nor did he move.

Rand took one step forward, wondering just how close he could get to the apparition. But as soon as his foot landed, the boy turned and walked out of sight around the corner. The IV pole's wheels squeaked as he went.

"Thomas, wait!" Rand broke into a run, but when he rounded the corner, the boy had disappeared.

"I know where he's taking you," Harold said.

Rand brought the radio to his mouth as he slowly proceeded down the hall. "Should I be afraid?"

"Don't go, Rand," Harold said. "Turn back. Your time's up, anyway."

"I can't do that. I'm close."

"I'm begging you. There has to be another way."

A boom sounded on Rand's left as if something heavy had fallen over. It had come from the other side of the door he'd just passed.

The sign on the wall said MORGUE.

22

Rand's breath caught. *I should've known.*

"I see what you mean," Rand said into the radio. "I'm guessing I need badge access."

"Of course."

"Help me out, Harold."

"Rand…"

"For Georgia."

The man was silent for a long time, and Rand wondered if their connection had been broken. But then, without a word from Harold, the badge scanner near the door handle blinked from red to green.

The light flickered on when he entered, motion activated. A metal examining table stood in the center of the room. Shelves of square boxes lined the walls like drawers in a filing cabinet. Each had a label with a name and identification number. Rand shivered—at first because the place gave him the creeps, but then he saw his breath frosting in front of his lips, and he knew he was not alone in that small room.

He circled back to the door and pushed against it. Stuck. Trapped inside. And this time, there was nowhere else to go.

"Stuck again, Harold," Rand said into the radio. "Maybe you can head down this way and let me out. I have a feeling by the time you get here I'll know what I need to know."

Rand looked around the room again, waiting for Thomas to make his next move. "I'm here. Show me what you want me to see."

Silence.

"I'm losing my patience with you. Enough of these games."

A loud, crashing sound came from behind him.

Rand whirled and saw the walled-in office of the morgue through a glass window. Everything had been swept off the desk and onto the floor by an invisible force.

"Trash the place if you want, Thomas, but you're not scaring me."

The hair rose on the back of his neck. He got the unmistakable impression he was being watched.

And when he turned, the apparition stood on the other side of the examining table, maybe six paces away. It was the boy from Georgia's picture, and he wore a simple hospital gown and gripped an IV pole with his right hand. A single line ran from his vein to the dripping bag that dangled above him. He stared at Rand with a blank expression, almost a glare.

"You don't need to be afraid," Rand whispered. "I'm here to help you."

The boy didn't budge. Rand still held the recorder, ready to pick up any speaking that came from Thomas.

It was then that Rand realized he'd never heard back from Harold.

"Harold," Rand said into the radio. "Are you there?"

"I'm here."

Thomas continued to stare at Rand, holding impossibly still.

"I need you to come let me out. We should be done by the time you get here."

"Can't do that," was all he said. The radio gave static feedback so thick it was hard to discern Harold's words.

Rand licked his lips. "Why's that?"

The feedback grew, and Rand tried to adjust the channel. It didn't help. The whole time, he kept an eye on the apparition, waiting for it to make a move.

"Harold, I'm losing you."

"Randolph Casey," Harold said through the noise, and his voice no longer sounded like his own. "Why don't you go fuck yourself?"

Thomas turned and put his back to Rand. His untied hospital gown hung open, revealing a gaping wound from Thomas's head to the top of his buttocks. His flesh was open, showing his bloody spinal cord, his guts, his organs.

And Rand knew he was in the presence of evil.

"In the name of Shindael," the radio said in a dark voice, and then he began speaking a language Rand had never heard before. It was not Harold. The entity before him was speaking through the radio.

"Leave here!" Rand shouted at Thomas's back. "I command you—"

Thomas's head twisted around. His eyes glowed blood red, and his face contorted in a grimace.

The voice on the radio spoke faster and louder,

jumbled and nonsensical words. Rand drew back and threw the radio right at Thomas, but the boy batted it away with impossible speed and strength. It shattered against the wall of freezers.

The drawer it hit sprung open by itself. Then another. Followed by a third.

Thomas's face no longer resembled a human, but a creature. Red eyes, razor teeth, and scaled skin replaced the guise of an innocent boy.

The drawers opened with such force that the bodies flew from their tables, landing on the floor like stiff, frozen blocks. Naked corpses rained around the room, tossed about by an invisible force.

A table containing a neat arrangement of medical instruments leapt an inch off the ground and fell. Rand spotted it just in time. He gripped the examining table and toppled it onto its side, dropping behind it.

An instant later, the instruments were flying right at him. Razors, speculums, needles, and scalpels. Their sharp points clanged on the other side of the examining table, some soaring over and hitting the wall behind him.

Although the radio was smashed, the entity still shouted at him in the unknown language. It had changed from Harold's voice to one that spoke with a growl, barking from a creature that did not exist in the natural world. It got so loud that Rand had to cover his ears, feeling like his eardrums would burst at any second.

He couldn't hear himself scream or speak or think. Could not put together the words needed to command the entity to leave.

The lights in the morgue flickered, and then blew out in a rain of sparks, plunging him in darkness.

And in that moment, the oppressive force of the creature in the room with him was too much. He'd never felt such weight, such despair, such *evil*. His only thought was that this must be what it was like for an insect as it was crushed.

And Rand knew he'd lost. It had happened so quickly, and—despite all his knowledge and experience—he'd finally met his match. Whoever this monster was, it was not Thomas, and it was stronger than Rand had ever anticipated.

Hands gripped Rand's arms, which he was using to cover his face. He knew the creature had grabbed him and would now drag him to hell, or eviscerate him, or dismember him. Maybe all three. He fought back against the strong grip, knowing eventually he would lose.

"Rand!"

It knew his name.

But Rand also knew its name. It had told him on the radio. "Shindael!" he shouted. "I command you to leave, Shindael!"

Cold palms gripped his face. "Rand!"

Rand slowly opened his eyes and blinked. Harold came into focus, the big man kneeling over him.

And as Rand regained his composure, the tension left his body, but he still shivered and trembled.

"What—"

His mouth was desperate to move, but he could not form words.

"Come on," Harold said. "Let's get you out of here."

The next thing Rand knew, he was scooped up like a baby, surprised by Harold's strength as he was thrown over the man's shoulder and carried away. Rand tried to protest that he could walk, but it only came out in a jumbled mess.

Because, in that moment, his brain could only process one singular name.

Shindael.

23

Time seemed to skip ahead. The next thing Rand knew, he was in a room he didn't recognize. Bright lights shone overhead. He was on a mattress, one that was soft but not comfortable.

His head ached and throbbed. There were people around. Gradually, his clarity and thoughts came back to him and images of the morgue and the entity flooded his mind.

He shot straight up, only to feel hands on his shoulders, pushing him down.

"Whoa now," Harold said. "Not so fast."

"Relax for a minute, Rand," Katie said.

He looked around. He was in a small hospital room, lying on a stretcher. Only Harold and Katie were with him, and the curtain was drawn over the entrance. He had no idea what time it was, or how long he had been there.

"Katie," Rand said.

"Shh," she said. "You've been hurt."

"What…"

"Our connection cut out as soon as you went—" Harold checked over his shoulder and lowered his voice. "Into the morgue. When I couldn't get you to answer, I came running. Had a feeling something was off—more off than usual—and I was right."

Rand remembered how the entity had impersonated Harold on the radio, and the mysterious language he had spoken. "Thanks for that. I think you saved my ass."

"Looked like it," Harold said. "Never seen a mess like that in my life." He shuddered. Rand recalled the stiff bodies thrown around the room.

"Save those security videos for me," Rand said.

Harold shook his head. "Already tried to play them back. All blank. Destroyed. Whatever was in there with you took care of that."

Katie put her hand on Rand's arm, a soft and comforting touch. "Rand. What happened?"

"It isn't a ghost," he said, wiping at his face. It was slick and greasy as if he'd been sweating a lot. "Never was."

"You mean—"

"We have a demonic presence here."

Harold looked back and forth between Rand and Katie, confused. "Excuse me?"

"Makes sense now that I think about it," Katie said.

"Yeah. Something strong enough to keep the spirits of the children trapped here. Powerful enough to levitate things around Georgia's room. Not to mention its ability to mimic Harold's voice, tamper with electronic equipment, and speak unknown languages."

"I don't get it," Harold said. "What's the difference between a ghost and a demon?"

"Where do we even begin?" Rand's brain pounded from a headache that had settled in the bottom of his skull. "There is no Thomas. It was a demonic entity pretending to be Thomas. He was trying to gain Georgia's trust, and he almost did."

"Until you came," Harold said.

"Yeah."

"Do you think you'll be the new target now?" Katie asked.

"Most likely." In all previous cases he'd worked on involving demonic infestations, Rand had become the target of the entity. That was fine with him. As long as the creature no longer concerned himself with Georgia Collins.

"Where am I?" Rand asked.

"In the emergency room," Katie told him. "Georgia's in the waiting area outside. She's worried about you."

"How nice."

"Rand," Katie said. "What do we do now? We have to get rid of this thing."

She was right. And now that they knew they were dealing with the demonic, their plan of attack had to change.

"We have to cleanse the children's ward and bless it. An exorcism."

"Exorcism?" Harold said, eyes wide. "That's a real thing?"

"More real than you'd probably like to believe," Rand told him. "It's not just for people, though. We use it to remove these entities from places as well." Then Rand remembered something. "My recorder. I lost it in the morgue."

"You mean this?" Harold held it up.

"Ah, good man." Rand took it from him and pressed play. He rolled the recording through the captured audio, hoping the demon's presence hadn't ruined the device. The recording was still intact, thankfully. "Listen to this," he told Katie. He found the part from the morgue, and the heavy, guttural voice came through the speaker. The garbled tongue of an unknown language.

Katie winced at the demon's words. "He must have been close. You can hear him without any amplification."

"That was the closest I've ever been to one," Rand said, shuddering at the memory. "And this one is powerful."

Shindael.

"And... he told me his name."

Katie frowned. "What?"

"Yeah. You heard me."

"Did you command him to tell you?"

"No. That's what's weird about it. He told me on his own like he wanted me to know."

Katie gave him a strange look. "I don't know, Rand. There's something off about that."

A demon's name was one of its biggest weaknesses. If you knew it, it was easier to take control over him and banish him back to hell. Demons went to great lengths to hide their names from those who sought to fight against them.

So why would he volunteer his name so easily?

The curtain was pulled aside, and a doctor entered carrying a chart of papers. "Mr. Casey, I see you're awake." Rand nodded but said nothing. He wondered what reason had been given for his check-in. "Have you ever fainted before?"

"No."

"I wouldn't worry too much. Probably just stress and fatigue. Take some time off work and relax a bit. If it happens again, make an appointment with a neurologist. I'll get your discharge papers ready."

The doctor and Harold exchanged a knowing look before he disappeared on the other side of the curtain.

"Fainting?" Rand asked him.

"Should I have told him you were attacked by a demon, instead? Besides, he knew why you were *really* in the hospital tonight."

"How many people around here know who I am and what I do?" If the word got around too much, that could interfere with his work.

"I told you, Rand. Many people in the hospital are experiencing things now. Whatever you saw in the morgue is getting stronger."

The curtain pulled open again, but this time it wasn't the doctor. It was a woman that Rand had never seen before, dressed in a brown pantsuit and her chestnut hair tied in a bun on the back of her head. She did not seem at all pleased to see him. Rand glanced at Harold, who looked at the newcomer with astonishment, which told Rand this lady was not on the same page. "Mr. Casey?"

"Who's asking?"

She took one step into the room and lifted his wrist. Someone had placed a white hospital wristband on him, stating his name and date of birth.

"I need a word with you, Mr. Casey, if we could have some privacy."

"I don't want to keep secrets from friends." Rand didn't like the intense and abrupt way in which the lady had conducted herself so far. She reminded him of Tessa's mother.

"I insist," she said. "Or, if you prefer, we could go ahead and call the police."

24

Katie eyed him, and Rand nodded. She stood and left. In that moment, he wished he still had access to Bill's open bar. He had a feeling he was going to need it.

"That will be all, Harold. Thank you," the woman said. "You can return to your post."

"Yes, ma'am."

Once they were alone, the woman pulled up the chair Katie had occupied. "My name is Fiona Shaw. I'm the director of the children's ward here at St. Mary's."

Her lips were pressed into a thin line and her cold blue eyes pierced him with a hard gaze. Rand figured all her subordinates cowered underneath that stare.

"Randolph Casey," he said, struggling to sit up on the stretcher. "My friends call me Rand. Religious Studies professor at—"

"I know who you are, Mr. Casey," Fiona said. "And what you do."

"Ah. A fan." He tried his best charming smile, but it did nothing to melt Fiona's frozen exterior.

"Hardly. I'll make this quick. After Dr. Carter has assembled your discharge papers, you will leave St. Mary's and not come back."

"Isn't that always the hope when one leaves the hospital?"

"Mr. Casey, I am very serious. I have added you to the blacklist and you are now banned from this facility. Your name has been distributed to all security and staff, and if you ever show your face here again the police will be called, and you will be arrested."

For the first time, Rand frowned. "Why are you doing this?"

"I'm doing what is best for this hospital and the patients."

He paused and met her gaze for a long time. She did not budge, as if they were playing a staring game. "And what is it you think I did to deserve this?"

"You are responsible for exacerbating rumors that this facility is 'haunted.' " She spat the word as if it tasted bad. "That is not true, and continuing assertions that it is cannot go on. We have lost too many staff members over these crazy tales, and more importantly, should news of this ever get out, it would be very detrimental to the institution. St. Mary's is known in the community as a faith-based healing center with a strong Catholic support system. We can't have the staff thinking ghosts are running around the place."

"Are you a practicing Catholic?" Rand asked. For the first time, Fiona Shaw let her rock-solid shield slip. But only for a moment. Rand took her reaction as a yes. "And you believe in spirits and demons, don't you?"

"This has nothing to do with me."

"It has everything to do with your hospital. Your healing center. Your patients are being tormented by a demonic entity. It has attached itself to Georgia Collins."

"Enough, Mr. Casey. You sound like a crazy person."

But Rand could see how her eyes darted when he'd said the D-word. Saw the way her hands wrung in her lap.

"I'm here to help you. And Georgia."

"Myself and the other directors have already discussed it. If Georgia Collins and her family keep spreading these rumors or engaging in this activity, we'll have to relocate her to a more appropriate place to continue her treatment."

"What? That's not fair. You can't punish her for this."

"This isn't punishment. It's protection for all the patients."

"Don't do this," Rand said. "I get it, you have a hospital to run. But you're letting your job get in the way of your better judgment." Fiona Shaw looked away again. "I'm the only one who can help you. If you don't address this now, it will only get worse. You already told me you know who I am and what I do, so trust me."

Fiona Shaw eyed him hard for what seemed like an eternity. Then she stood and pulled the curtain aside. "I'll check with Dr. Carter and see what's taking him so long with the discharge papers. Remember what I told you, Mr. Casey. I'd hate for us to have an incident in the future."

Rand fell back onto the stretcher and rubbed at his eyes. The headache wouldn't go away and fatigue coursed through every inch of his body. He knew he needed to sleep, but he also wouldn't be able to until the job was done.

The job, which had gotten much more difficult now that he was no longer allowed inside St. Mary's. Rand was accustomed to getting kicked out of places, but this time his banishment was dangerous to others. Without him, Georgia Collins was vulnerable. And since the demon was out of hiding, his attacks would only become more vicious.

Shindael.

When the doctor returned, Rand snatched up the discharge papers and didn't wait around to hear what he had to say.

Katie and Georgia met him in the waiting room. "Who was that lady?" Katie asked.

"We need to make a plan, and now," Rand told her. "We don't have much time."

25

R and wobbled down the hall on rubbery legs, the feeling still had not fully returned to his body. Aches and pains lingered with him, and Fiona Shaw's banishment had been the final kick to put him down.

But he would not lose hope.

"A demon," Georgia said as she and Katie followed behind him. He was limping, like an injured fighter after a beating, and they kept pace with him patiently. "So, you're saying it wasn't Thomas at all."

"No," Rand said. "You were never talking with your friend."

The hospital was starting to wake up. Night-shift nurses were on the way out, looking tired and haggard. The early visitors had appeared, and The Coffee Bean was brewing the day's first batch. A pleasant smell wafted down the corridor, but the thought of having a coffee only made Rand's stomach churn.

"But... it looked just like him."

"They can imitate well," Rand said. "But never perfectly. There is always some kind of flaw." Rand remembered the gashed-open spinal cord from the morgue.

"Now that you mention it," Georgia said. "I could never see his legs. When he appeared, he seemed invisible from the waist down. But why pretend to be Thomas?"

"To gain your trust."

"And after that?"

Rand halted when he walked by the chapel. The door was open, and the inside was dark, like a portal to a different holy dimension within the hospital. And in that moment, Rand felt its strong draw.

"That's the chapel," Georgia said. "Remember? We passed by it the first day you came."

"Are you going in?" Katie asked, concerned. She knew how every time he encountered the demonic, the only thing he wanted to do afterward was get into the presence of God.

"Yeah. I have to."

"Didn't take you for a big man of faith, Ghost Man," Georgia said.

"It's something I have to do. I'll be in touch with you later, okay? Keep your phone charged."

"Am I in, like, a lot of trouble?"

"You're in danger," Rand told her bluntly.

Georgia chewed her lip. "Can you help me?"

"Yes, but first I need to prepare. Then I'll come back as soon as I can."

"But they banned you."

"Does that seem like the kind of thing that'll stop me?"

"Good point, Ghost Man. Just please don't forget

about me here. I'm officially scared now." She fist-bumped him and walked away, rolling her oxygen tank behind her.

"Nice girl," Katie said when she was gone. "Now I see why you're so serious about helping her."

"So when I come back, will you join me?"

"I have to," Katie said. "This one seemed to take a lot out of you. It's a powerful presence, and you can't do it by yourself. Or maybe you're just getting old."

"I've never felt anything like it before," Rand said, trying to keep the memory from surfacing again. The presence alone had been so intense it may have killed him if Harold hadn't come for him. "This shouldn't take long," he said, pointing a thumb at the chapel. "Wait for me in the coffee shop—have breakfast or whatever. Then I'll bring you home."

"You want anything?"

"The last thing I want right now is to eat." He placed a hand over his belly, which felt like he had ingested a large stone.

Inside, the chapel resembled a miniature Catholic church. There were pews on either side of the aisle, five on each. At the back was an altar, a table, and a wall-mounted crucifix with Jesus looking down over the sanctuary.

No one had stopped by for morning prayers, giving Rand a welcome solace. The room was colder than the hallway outside and had a pleasant smell of finished wood. Stained-glass windows along the sides depicted Bible scenes. The lights were pleasantly dim in the early hours.

Rand limped down the aisle and sat on the front pew, looking up at the cross and the statue of Jesus.

Rand's involvement with religion had always been complicated. He'd been raised Catholic by a strict mother, lapsed in high school, and forgotten all about it until he'd gotten involved in his current line of work. Now, his relationship with God was strained. He wondered why, if God was all-powerful, he allowed the demons to torment innocent people. Surely with a wave of his hand, he could eradicate them forever. Still, he chose not to. His own life had been irreparably altered. This left him angry at God, but whenever he encountered the demonic, as he had a few hours ago, nothing felt right until he fell before the Lord and sanctified himself.

That made him feel like a hypocrite who only needed God when he faced true evil and thought he could handle all other problems on his own.

But Rand owned that completely. He had seen the minions of hell. After that, it seemed benign to pray about anything else that happened in his life.

"There is evil here," Rand whispered to the statue in prayer. "Give me the strength needed to save this girl and her family. I ask that you help me help her."

Although he was experienced, Rand always felt self-doubt when going head-to-head with the demonic. There was no force on earth more unpredictable.

"Good morning."

The strong voice startled him from behind, interrupting his prayer. Rand stood and turned. There, he faced an older man who wore a black suit and a white clerical collar around his neck.

"Good morning," Rand said.

The man strolled down the aisle, appraising him. Rand got the feeling that the priest knew who he was.

"Do you know me?" Rand asked.

"No," he said. "But I know what you are."

The headache still lingered in the base of his skull. "A lot of people have been telling me that. I'm worried that it'll soon go to my head."

"People talk in this hospital. You come to visit Georgia Collins, and I'm aware of the things she's been seeing. It's been a long time since she's come down to Mass."

"I'll remind her that going to Mass is highly recommended during times like this." He held out his hand. "Randolph Casey. Friends call me Rand."

The priest clasped it, almost too tight, as if he'd been desperate for another human's touch. "Father Calvin. I understand the family brought you in because of the ghost stories."

"Yes."

"And that you did indeed find a ghost."

"I wish," Rand said. "What I found was worse. A distinguished man of God such as yourself should know what I'm talking about."

Father Calvin only stared at him, a hardness coming across his face like a shield going up.

"She needs you," Rand said.

"I cannot help her." He looked away.

"You must have sensed what was here long before I ever came. Felt it."

"I don't feel much of anything these days," Father Calvin said. "My job is here in the chapel."

"The real job will never be just inside this chapel. And you know it."

"I don't meddle with such things anymore," Calvin

said. "I did once in my youth, and it was then that I learned I am not strong enough."

"You are responsible for these patients," Rand said. "There must be something you can do."

Calvin looked at him for a long while, hard and silent. "Let's speak frankly, then. You are talking about an exorcism."

"Yes. This hospital is infested with a demonic spirit. It seems anchored to the tenth ward, specifically—drawn there. It's grown stronger over time, and now that I've come and challenged it directly, it will only become more dangerous."

"I cannot help you," Calvin said.

"Why?"

Calvin sat down in the pew as if he were suddenly too weak to stand. "Twenty years ago, I assisted in an exorcism. It was the only one I have ever been involved with. It was a little girl possessed by a demon named..." He trailed off. "No. I will not name him. But I will never forget the name, or the face of the girl as it invaded her body. He beat her and broke her, pulled out her hair, scarred her. The vulgarities and blasphemies that came out of her mouth were unlike anything I'd ever heard. It took four full days of constant fighting to cast that monster out of her. After that, I knew I could never do it again. It was just too much. I was so weak, so demoralized. For days afterward, I had dreams of hanging myself or jumping off the roof of a tall building. I decided that kind of work was not for me, yet I felt horrible because it seemed it was the highest calling of any man of God. Here I was, content to sit inside a confession booth or give sermons on Sundays. Meanwhile, the real God-fearing men were out there tackling true evil." Calvin looked up at him, and Rand got the impression he was the only one to have ever heard this tale. "But what could I do? I tried once, and it nearly forced me to end my own life. I am not carved from stone like those other priests. God did not give me the same constitution, and surely he would not require it from all of his devoted disciples."

Rand sat in the pew across the aisle. He felt for the man—truly did. He remembered his first brush with the demonic, all those years ago. He'd gone through the same trauma, the same pain, and had come out on the other side as a changed person. He'd known he could no longer go through life ignoring the evil that lurked in the corners of the most innocent and unsuspecting places.

"How did you pull through?" Rand asked.

"Through the grace of God alone."

"So you're okay sitting back and watching the demonic encroach on your territory? On your patients and your flock?"

Father Calvin said nothing. Only looked at the floor between his feet.

"Would you try again? For Georgia and her family?"

"I don't know *what* I'm willing to do anymore," Calvin said. "I've considered that maybe there is nothing we can do. That things will happen as they may, without our control."

"Isn't that called God's plan?"

"Yes, if you're the cynical type. I've seen so many patients come and go in this hospital. Some walk out, some never leave. No matter what prayers I say, very little seems to get answered in the way we ask. So what's the point? Maybe there really is no one listening."

"Now is not the time to lose faith," Rand said, although he felt ridiculous saying it. At the best of times, his own belief was about as solid as a house of cards, something he only cashed in on during situations of desperate need.

"No one chooses to lose their faith, Rand. So I imagine the timing is even more out of our control."

It was hard for Rand to argue. Watching patients die after praying so earnestly for their healing had to take its toll. Such were the mysteries of God, though. Some lived while others died. Some walked and others were crippled. And all the while, inhuman evil spirits ran wild on his flock.

Rand stood from the pew. "I'm coming back soon. When I do, I will remove this spirit from this place. The more people we have fighting for Georgia, the better. I hope I can count on you to join and that you can muster up enough faith for this. It could be the biggest battle of your life."

Father Calvin's face was heavy and sad as he frowned. He looked like he wanted to say something, but just couldn't find the words.

26

The bell jingled over the door when Rand walked in.

The used bookshop was in disarray. Boxes of paperbacks were open and resting in the walkways, big cardboard tripping hazards. Other stacks of books weren't in boxes at all but piled on the tables and the floor and even by the cash register. A thin layer of dust lingered in the air, tickling Rand's nose and threatening to make him sneeze.

He made his way to the counter while stepping over the boxes, making him walk like he was in quicksand. Something crashed to the ground in the closet behind the counter, and someone muttered a curse.

"What's the point of having the bell over the door if you ignore it?" Rand said.

"What's the point of shouting at me when you can clearly see—oh." Miller stuck his head out and finally saw who had entered his stop. "Rand Casey, the one and only." Miller dropped whatever he was holding with a crash and dusted his hands off as he walked out of the closet. "I didn't know you were coming so soon."

"You got my message, right?"

"With all those audio files? Yeah, of course."

Rand looked around at the disorganized state of the place. "Have you had time to look into it, or have you been distracted with all this spring cleaning?"

"It's fall. And I'm not cleaning. You know how much I hate to clean. I'm just trying to reorganize. The stacks have gone crazy on me."

"Or you've been negligent."

"If it weren't unethical to charge for my side gig, I wouldn't have to worry about running this dump."

"So you had time to look at the files?"

"Let's step into my office."

Miller Landingham was a head shorter than Rand and far more overweight than the last time Rand had seen him. His neck and chin sported a healthy orb of fat that spread his already-thin stubble. His black hair was disheveled and greasy, matching the thick rims of his glasses, which made his eyes pop. He almost always wore a button-up, plaid, short-sleeve shirt and khaki pants, and he walked with a deep limp from an injury that Rand had been present for long ago.

The two never would have become acquaintances in real life if Miller's unfortunate brush with the demonic hadn't brought them together years before.

"Even after all this time, the stuff you send me still freaks me out."

"Come on. Where's the professionalism?"

"Don't tell me it doesn't get to you, too. Keep in mind I'm listening to this by myself in here after hours."

He opened the door to the bookshop's back office. It was uncomfortably warm inside, and besides the usual desk and computer and overflowing filing cabinet, there was a brown mattress pushed against the far wall with a single bedspread and a flattened pillow. Crumpled fast-food wrappers and empty soda cans were accumulating around it.

"You're really committed to the overtime."

"Larry spiked the rent on my place last month. Can you believe it? The man's always been a dirtbag."

"So you live here now?"

"I'm crashing until I figure something else out."

Miller sat heavily in the chair at his desk, making the cracked leather groan and letting out a puff of air from the seat. He jiggled the mouse and the computer came to life. "So this Shindael. Yeah, there's a lot on him. He's been busy the past couple of years. Where did I put it?"

Miller rummaged through a pile beside the monitor—invoices, shipping receipts, and overdue bill notices—until he found a stack of papers he'd paper-clipped together. "Here it is. Printed out every instance where I ran across his name on the web."

Rand skimmed through the documents. The printouts were from message boards, online forums, and niche websites that Miller owned and moderated—places where people recounted their own personal accounts of the demonic.

Rand knew well that Miller did not want to face a demonic entity again in person, but he wanted to help out after Rand had rescued him from an intelligent haunting a few years before. The way he did that was by scouring the darkest corners of the internet for information people posted on their own encounters, then saved it all in a large file. It contained eyewitness accounts and personal experiences, and he cross-referenced them for similarities and grouped them together. If one account determined a demon's name, then Miller could match it with other similar stories and discover a type of "MO" for that particular demon. Knowing whom you were dealing with gave you the upper hand in any battle with the demonic.

He also used this information to create a database of known demons and their names—as well as their appearances when someone was unlucky enough to glimpse one in their true form. All of it was like a modern-day grimoire, he'd said once, and Rand had to admit that the data had been useful to him on more than a few occasions.

"And you've vetted the crazies?" Rand asked.

"As much as I could. You'll see all those accounts have at least a few similarities. There are three or four mediums who managed to speak with him. Apparently, he is quite talkative and receptive and usually shows up quickly when called by name." Miller shivered. "Freaks me out just to think about."

Rand thumbed through the pages. The stories were long and drawn out, so he'd have to sit down and read through them later.

"The short version is, he's a high ranker," Miller said. Rand looked up at him. "Yeah. The real deal. There are several demons that are under him, or are his slaves, or servants, or whatever. I saw one account of someone who was able to send away Rakhon-om simply by threatening to invoke Shindael. You remember Rakhon-om?"

"He's a rotten piece of work. But why would Shindael

tell me his name?" Rand said, flipping the stack of papers closed. "That doesn't make any sense. These bastards do anything they can to keep me from learning their names. But this one, Shindael, he wanted me to know."

"Because he's an arrogant prick would be my guess," Miller said. "He commands other demons. He ranks in hell. Wouldn't you think you were awesome too?"

"Perhaps."

"Also, get this. Those recordings you sent me…"

"Yeah? You figured them out?"

"It wasn't so simple as Latin or backward English. I had to ship that off to my linguist friend at the university, and then she had to pass it along when even *she* couldn't place it."

"And?"

Miller leaned back in his chair, proud of himself. "Ancient Sumerian."

Rand stared at him.

"I thought you'd be confused," Miller said. He spun and made a few clicks on his computer. He played the audio file Rand had sent him—the recording of Shindael yelling in his deep voice in the morgue, the words unrecognizable.

"Sumer was a civilization in Mesopotamia around three thousand BC," Miller said. "Modern-day Iraq. One of the first to exist. They spoke their own Sumerian language, but it only lasted about a thousand years before intermingling with other civilizations caused Akkadian to become the primary spoken language in the area."

"So in other words, he's showing off."

"That was also my conclusion."

Shindael was probably trying to impress upon Rand

how timeless he was. Show how long he'd been watching humans, tormenting them.

"How's the girl?" Miller asked.

"All right for now," Rand said while rubbing at his eyes, exhaustion setting in. "They kicked me out of the hospital, so I have to find a way back to her if I'm going to help."

"Hang in there," Miller said, standing from the chair. "Read those Shindael encounters I printed out for you. See if you can get any useful information."

"Will do."

"And be careful. If this gets nasty and you need any assistance, give me a call."

"But you hate the front line."

"I do. But I have a bad feeling about this one, this Shindael. He seems like a real son of a bitch, so just... watch your back."

27

S tacy Thompson was the last one to hand in her quiz. She always checked and rechecked it, making sure her answers were correct. Rand didn't even have to grade her work against the answer key to know she got a hundred percent.

The girl seemed oddly interested in this stuff. Not something he would have ever expected from someone like her.

She rose from her usual desk at the front of the classroom and passed her paper to him. "Thank you, Stacy," Rand said. "I'm sure it's an A as always."

"I don't know," she said, frowning. "This was harder than the rest."

It wasn't. It was one of the easiest quizzes on his syllabus. As long as she hadn't overthought it, she'd be fine.

He stuffed her quiz in the stack along with the others and shoveled them into his bag. He closed his laptop and put it inside his case. Stacy didn't move.

"Anything else I can help you with?"

"No, sir," she began, although Rand could tell she had something she needed to say. "It's just that... you seem off."

"Off?"

"Yeah. Distracted, spaced out. I don't know. Is everything all right?"

No. Everything was not all right. Stacy was quite perceptive. Georgia Collins and the case at hand had dominated his thoughts lately, as they tended to do, and he was trying his best to keep that from spilling over into his lectures.

"Just some stuff going on right now," he said.

"Like what you talk about in your class?" She gestured toward the screen where he projected his photos of previous cases, hauntings, and demons.

"Yeah."

"That sounds scary," Stacy said. "Please be careful."

"Thank you, Stacy."

Once he was alone in the classroom, he scooped up his stuff and bounded for the door.

He almost ran into someone as they were coming in.

"Excuse me," Rand blurted out and tried to maneuver around the lady in his way.

"Mr. Casey."

A familiar voice. He turned and saw that the person he'd almost bumped into was Doris Galloway, the woman who'd audited his class and wanted to remove it from the university curriculum.

"Afternoon," he said, trying to keep his tone pleasant, but he couldn't afford to think about this right now.

"Sorry I ran into you. I'm in a hurry, actually. Is there any way this could—"

"This isn't about the audit," Doris said, stepping closer to him and keeping her voice low. Her face was not stern and inquisitive, as it had been in their previous meeting.

"Oh. What can I help you with, then?" Rand checked his watch.

"The little girl," she said, glancing around them as if she did not want to be overheard. "The one who that couple came to see you about?"

"Yeah?" Rand said, curiosity piqued.

"Is she... okay?" She looked genuinely concerned.

"Not yet. But I'm working with her."

Doris nodded as if she'd been given a bad health diagnosis. "Right. Sorry, it's just that ever since then I've been thinking about it. And about her."

"It's complicated at the moment."

"I understand. Well, I don't, but... I'm just hoping you can help that family."

"I appreciate your concern." Rand smiled.

Doris nodded. Then she straightened herself and her professional mask returned. "That will be all, Mr. Casey."

———

LIBBY STEPPED out of the elevator on the tenth floor, expecting to be greeted by Harold's friendly smile, but instead it was another man at the security desk.

"Where's Harold? Is he off today?" she asked as she signed in.

"Harold's been suspended," said the man—whose name was Jerry, according to his badge.

"Oh." Libby frowned as she placed the name tag on her shirt. She surmised that had happened because he'd helped her dad.

Libby had never before gotten so involved with one of her dad's cases. But something about Georgia was different. She was a girl Libby could see herself being friends with after this whole mess was over. No one ever deserved to be tormented by a demonic spirit, but Georgia was an especially vulnerable victim. She found herself eager to help in any way she could, so when she'd gotten a text from Georgia an hour before asking her to come and visit, she'd called Justin and canceled their date so she could go.

When Libby entered the nurse station, she stopped short in her tracks. Georgia Collins, her parents, Nurse Donna, three more nurses, and four other children—patients, Libby assumed—formed a circle near the desk, hands joined, heads bowed.

"And lead us not into temptation, but deliver us from evil," Nick Collins intoned. "For thine is the Kingdom, and the power, and glory forever."

Georgia caught Libby's eye and gestured with her head for her to come and join them. Libby walked over and broke into the circle between Georgia and a nurse and clasped their hands.

"There is evil here, Lord," Nick continued in prayer. "We have all been affected by it, and some have seen it. Please intervene and reclaim this place in your name. We are your children, and we dedicate our lives to you. Please rescue us from this creature from hell and give us the courage needed to see through its deceptions."

As Mr. Collins prayed, Libby felt Georgia's hand squeeze hers tighter and tighter, as if afraid to let go.

It had been a long time since Libby had prayed, and in a way she felt as if she did not belong in such a devout circle. But she understood the desperate times these people were facing and kept her head bowed respectfully.

That was until a sharp voice interrupted them from the other side of the room.

"That will be enough."

Nick Collins's prayer was cut short, as if with a knife. There stood a tall and ferocious-looking woman wearing a brown pantsuit, with dark hair tied into a tight bun. Her eyes were ice as she approached the circle, her heels clacking against the tile.

"Miss Shaw," Nurse Donna began, but the woman only held out her hand.

"You know I support prayer and prayerful gatherings. But they are to be done in the appropriate venue and at the appropriate times. There is a very nice chapel on the first floor available to all of our patients." She eyed Donna and the other nurses. "And prayer times should be restricted to your one-hour break. Doing this while on the clock is negligent to the other patients."

Donna looked like she had a great deal of things to say to the frigid woman, but in the end, she acquiesced. "Yes, ma'am."

The prayer circle fell apart like a wilting flower. The nurses returned to the desk and the other children meandered back to their rooms.

Libby had heard about this woman from her dad. Fiona Shaw, the director of the children's ward, had confronted him and banned him from the hospital.

Fiona stood her ground and watched everyone fade away. Then, she fixed Georgia Collins in her stern gaze. "I'm glad to see you getting back into your faith, Miss Collins," Shaw said as she approached. "Father Calvin has noted your absence from his services lately. But as I said, there is a time and a place for that. There is an appropriate way to go about it." As Shaw spoke, Georgia stared daggers at the woman, standing straight and defiant, as if her condition did not leave her body weak and broken. "And I do not appreciate you spreading stories that scare the staff and the other patients."

"They're not stories," Georgia said, her words sharp. "I know what I've seen, and everyone here knows what they've experienced."

Nick put his hand on his daughter's shoulder and squeezed, but it did nothing to make her back down.

"I'm sorry," Nick Collins offered. "We've spent so much time here that this place almost feels like our living room. We'll keep the prayers inside from now on."

"I'm *not* sorry," Georgia said. "I know what's going on here, even if you refuse to believe it."

"Georgia," Maria said, a warning tone in her voice.

Georgia let out a loud groan, grabbed her portable oxygen cylinder, and stormed off down the corridor.

Fiona Shaw then fixed Libby with her steel-blue eyes. "And you—Libby Casey, according to the visitor log. I won't hesitate to ban you from this facility if you cause even a fraction of the trouble your father stirred up. You can consider this your first and final warning."

With that, Fiona Shaw turned and left.

"Nasty woman," Libby said when she was out of earshot.

"She just doesn't understand," Nick Collins said. "Come on."

They caught up with Georgia in her room, where she was replacing her empty oxygen tank with a full one.

"I don't get it, Dad," Georgia said as soon as they walked in. "Why do you act all weak in front of her? She's the worst, and she doesn't believe anything that's happened!"

"It's her ward, Georgia," Nick said calmly. "We have to play by her rules."

But Libby remembered what her dad had told her. Shaw had threatened to remove Georgia from the hospital if she kept scaring the other patients. Surely Nick and Maria had been warned as well.

"There *are* no rules anymore," Georgia said. "Not when something like this is going on."

Her anger spike caused her to lose her breath, and she started to cough. She sat down, weakened by the spasm, and hacked her lungs into a tissue for several minutes before she could get her breathing under control.

"Don't wind yourself up too much," Libby said, rubbing Georgia's back. "Everything will work out okay."

Georgia wiped the tears from the corners of her eyes. "How? Your dad isn't allowed in here. How's he going to help me?"

"I don't have an answer for that," Libby said. "But one thing I know for sure is that my dad has never given up on a client. Not ever. No matter how bad it gets, he always wins. Now, let's forget about that Fiona Shaw lady and go downstairs for some ice cream."

Georgia took deep breaths and seized control of her

breathing again. "You know just what to say to cheer a girl up. How did you know her name anyway?"

"Because my dad had plenty of terrible things to call her when he got home yesterday."

"I'm sure every word was true. Come on. If we hurry, we can get there before Mrs. Eloise's shift is over. Then the ice cream will be free."

28

Thunder rolled heavy and loud in the distance. The glass rattled in the window panes from the vibrations.

Rachel pulled the curtain aside and looked out into the dark night, a worried expression on her face. "What are the odds that your power will go out?"

"I think we'll be good," Rand said, not entirely sure if it was true.

"Because I really want to watch this movie with you," Rachel said. "I've been waiting a while, but you've been so busy lately."

Rand grabbed her and guided her down to the couch. "Nothing is going to stop us from watching this movie tonight," Rand said.

Rachel had been the unintended recipient of everything that had happened so far. Rand only had one goal for the night, and that was to make Rachel comfortable, put her mind at ease, and settle her frazzled nerves from all the stories about Georgia Collins.

Regardless, he knew the girl and her family would remain at the forefront of his thoughts.

During the first scene in the movie, Rand's phone buzzed.

"Who is that?" Rachel asked.

"Libby. She's hanging out with Georgia tonight."

Rachel frowned. He shouldn't have brought it up. "Is everything okay?" she asked, even though Rand knew she didn't really want to know.

Rand did not reply. He laid his phone face down and leaned back on the couch with Rachel as they watched the movie. She cuddled into him, burying her face into his chest. He put his arm around her shoulders, holding her tight, but after watching for a few more minutes, Rand looked down at her and noticed that her eyes were not on the screen.

"What's the matter?" he asked.

"I don't know," Rachel said, sighing. "I have to pee." She got off the couch and disappeared into the back hallway.

The movie would not make her feel better. It wasn't enough of a distraction from everything that had been going on.

He lifted the remote and paused the movie. The only sound in the living room was the wind outside and the coming storm.

Then three loud knocks on the door.

Rand sat up straight, suddenly alert, an anxious feeling clenching inside his stomach. He stood and crept to his bag, which rested against the far wall, and pulled out a wooden crucifix, the one he brought with him to every investigation.

He held it out toward the door, staring it down,

waiting to see if whatever was on the other side knocked again. He gripped the doorknob and flung it open.

There was nobody there.

He stuck his head out. The front yard was shrouded in the dark night, the sky marred by rolling, grey storm clouds.

His palms grew clammy. These occurrences were very familiar to him.

Rand went back inside, then closed the door and locked it. The only light in the room came from the luminescent television screen, the movie paused in a single frame.

Suddenly, Rand got the impression he was not alone in the house. Not because of Rachel in the bathroom. No, someone or something was with him in the living room. He felt eyes on him.

"I command you to leave here," Rand said, turning in circles, the cross still raised, keeping his attention on all corners of the room.

Loud thumps overhead. As if someone were running along the roof.

This demon was escalating things faster than usual. It had taken no time at all to follow Rand home.

This was a standard occurrence. Once Rand stirred up a spirit enough, the entity would always come after him rather than his initial target. That was good. If the demon left Georgia Collins alone for at least a little while, she would get a reprieve.

Then there was a loud crash at the back of the house, and his heart leapt into his throat.

Rand rushed down the hall and threw open the door on the right—his office.

Inside, he found the entire room ransacked.

His desk was overturned, books had been thrown from the shelves, and pictures had been torn from the walls, the frames smashed on the ground. The window that looked out into the backyard was open as if a burglar had snuck in.

Just like the nurse station at the hospital.

Then Rachel screamed.

Rand rushed to the bathroom connected to his bedroom. He turned the knob, but the door did not open. He tried to force his way in, but it would not give. Something was holding it closed from the other side.

"Rachel!" Rand shouted as he banged on the door with his palm.

"Rand, help me!" she shrieked.

Rand stood back and kicked the door as hard as he could, cracking the wood and sending it flying open.

He ran inside just in time to see Rachel levitating in the air before she fell. Before the demon dropped her.

Rand caught her as best he could, and they both went down together. She wrapped her arms around him, squeezing him tight, her tears rubbing along his cheeks. Her chest heaved as she panted, her face red, her skin covered in slick sweat.

He clutched her tightly, knowing that he had brought this upon her. The entity was using Rachel to take revenge on him for provoking him.

"Rand—what was that? What's going on?"

Rand stroked her back as he held her. He still gripped the crucifix in his other hand.

She flinched.

"What?"

Rachel pulled the shirt down off her left shoulder, and he gasped at what she saw.

Three jagged wounds, red and glistening, resembling claw marks. Almost identical to his own scars on his back, an everlasting memento from a demonic foe.

"Rand, what the hell is this?" When she tried to touch them, she only flinched again, her fingers darting away from the pain as if the marks burned her.

Rand stared at the scratches, his jaw set, anger rushing through him for the first time.

Come after me all you want. But leave the others alone.

However, this was how it always worked. These entities knew him well, and often the best way to get to him was to go after his loved ones. Libby had had a very tumultuous childhood.

"I don't want to be here anymore," Rachel said through her tears.

"Come on. I'll take you home." Rand stood and helped her to her feet. She wobbled like her knees were made of jelly. Rand remembered how he felt the night he'd first encountered Shindael in the morgue.

You son of a bitch. As soon as I drop her off, I'm coming for you.

This demon was strong, and he was fast. There was no lurking and waiting with this one. He had to be removed tonight. There would be no peace until it was done.

29

It was eight-thirty in the evening, and the first floor of the hospital, which was usually crowded with patients, visitors, and medical professionals, had grown thin.

"How have you been?" Libby ventured as they walked. Georgia only shrugged in response. "I see you've ramped up the prayers."

"I'm not the only person having experiences anymore," Georgia said. "The nurses are all complaining. He keeps trashing their desk and throwing their charts all around. Someone grabs them and pushes them when they're walking down the hall at night, but there's no one there. A nurse named Nica already quit over it."

Libby remembered her dad telling her about Nica. He'd seen security footage of her getting tormented by the entity during her night shifts. It didn't help that Nica had already been a deep believer in the spiritual and super-natural.

"And now Fiona is on a rampage. I've never liked that woman."

"She seems kind of mean," Libby said.

"Yeah. And she totally believes us when we tell her these stories—I know she does. But it's all about the hospital image. All about the reputation. All about burying the problems so she doesn't get in trouble. And now she's banned your dad from ever coming back."

"I wouldn't worry about it too much," Libby said, trying to be consoling. "If you can believe it, my dad's banned from a lot of places." Georgia chuckled. "He always finds a way in."

Just then, Georgia stopped dead in her tracks. She stared straight ahead, her eyes growing wide and her mouth falling open.

"Georgia?" Libby followed her gaze down the corridor but saw nothing.

"Do you see him?" Georgia whispered.

"Who?"

Libby looked again, and then she saw.

A teenage boy dressed in a hospital gown. He gripped an IV pole next to him, and there was a bag of fluids running from the tube into a cannula in his arm.

Libby pulled Georgia close. She'd seen apparitions plenty of times in her life, and it was something she'd never gotten used to. A dark aura exuded from the boy all the way at the other end of the corridor.

"What do we do?" Georgia whispered.

Neither of them took their eyes off it as it glared at them. It held impossibly still. A standoff.

"It'll leave," Libby said, hoping that was true. Her mind

raced with all the ways her father had taught her to order a spirit to depart.

"Make him go away. Do something."

Command him, Libby thought at last. *Give him a command in the name of God and he has to listen.*

The lights in the corridor shut off and the backups came on, leaving them in a shadowy prison. There was no one else around, even though the area they were in was public. It was as if the demon had singled them out.

And then the boy walked toward them. The only sound was the squeaky wheels of his IV pole, steadily growing louder as he neared.

Georgia trembled against Libby's body and they clasped each other's hands. "Do something," she whispered again.

As the boy drew closer, Libby found her voice. "In the name of Jesus Christ, I command you to leave!"

He only smirked.

So there was only one thing left Libby could think to do—run.

"Come on!" She pulled Georgia's hand and forced her to turn around to run.

But as soon as they whirled, the boy in the hospital gown was there, a single pace away from them, the same smirk on his face.

The two girls let out a scream and stumbled backward.

The boy spoke to them, but the words were in a language that Libby could not understand. His voice was deep and unnatural, like a recording that had been ruined.

Libby pulled Georgia's hand as they ran the other way. This time, the boy did not appear in front of them. But as they fled, his words followed them down the corridor, booming after them. And although Libby could not understand, she also knew she did not want to.

Libby hoped they would find someone else who could help them. But the place seemed impossibly empty as if they had been transported to another dimension. Their hands remained clasped together, Georgia's oxygen cylinder bouncing up and down on its wheels.

They turned the corner and stopped short. The boy was there, except this time his back faced them. A gaping wound from his head to the top of his buttocks exposed a bloody spinal cord.

Georgia coughed. A hand went to her chest, her eyes bulged.

Libby knew they couldn't keep running away. Georgia's lungs wouldn't take it. Maybe that was what the demon wanted. Chase them until she dropped dead.

"Where's the chapel?" Libby said.

"I can't breathe," Georgia said between pants.

In front of them, the boy had turned around and stalked toward them again, the same grin on his darkened face.

"The chapel," Libby said, grasping Georgia by both arms. "We'll be safe in there!"

Georgia nodded. "This way."

They ran away from him again, Georgia mustering her breath as she led the way. They turned another corner, only to find the boy had appeared in front of them again.

But Georgia ran straight toward him while Libby followed. Libby panicked, hoping that Georgia knew where she was going. Then, Georgia yanked her into a room on the right.

The chapel was empty and dark. Libby slammed the door closed.

Surely we are okay in here. They can't enter holy places. At least, that was what her dad always told her.

Georgia fell onto her hands and knees, coughing and hacking. Libby crouched beside her, rubbing her back and stroking her hair. "It's okay. We're safe in here." She spotted the large crucifix mounted on the wall behind the altar. On it, Jesus looked up and away, lost in a daze of pain and defeat as he hung from the cross.

"Shit," Georgia muttered. She fumbled with the knob on her oxygen tank. The needle on the meter was in the red. "I can't stay in here for long."

"But... I saw you get a new one upstairs."

"I did! Something's wrong with it."

Libby figured the entity had something to do with that. "I'll call someone." She pulled out her phone.

"Are we really safe?" Georgia whispered.

"Yes. Demons can't come inside a holy—"

The door burst open as if hit by a wrecking ball. Both girls screamed and whirled around. The boy stood at the edge of the threshold into the chapel, his smile gone and replaced by an angry scowl.

He shouted at them again in the same mysterious language.

"Help us!" Libby called at the top of her lungs.

The boy pointed at them. Then, the stained-glass windows on either side of the room shattered all at the same time. The cushions in the pews ripped open by themselves, clouds of cotton drifting into the air, and the mounted Jesus statue unhooked from the wall and fell forward, crashing into the altar, and then to the ground, breaking into pieces. The lights above blew out, raining down shards of glass.

Amidst the destruction, Libby and Georgia hugged each other and dropped down. Libby threw herself over Georgia as the chapel fell apart around them, trying to shield the girl from any flying debris. She clenched her eyes, doing her best to pray for God's protection, but the commotion and the demon's chanting were the only things that filled her head.

Only after the room finally fell silent did Libby open her eyes. The chapel was completely trashed. No piece of furniture had been spared. Even the paint on the walls had been marred, covered in sets of three gouges like a giant claw had scratched them.

The boy was gone.

Libby helped Georgia to her feet. "Are you okay? Are you hurt?"

Georgia looked at her without seeing her, dazed. She stared for several long moments as if trying to think of what to say. Then she whispered, "It's over."

"What? What's over?"

Georgia collapsed into Libby's arms. The girl was dead weight, and Libby lowered her gingerly to the ground. "Georgia?" Libby gripped her shoulders and shook her. "Georgia, wake up!"

But she was unresponsive.

Libby did not know what to do. Start chest compressions? Shake her until she opened her eyes?

In the end, she ran out of the chapel and into the hallway, screaming for help.

30

The rain pelted down on them as they jogged to Rand's Jeep in the driveway. Once inside, Rand could no longer see the tears on Rachel's face mixed in with the rainwater.

As they drove, Rachel said nothing for a long while. The only sounds were the drops pattering on the windshield and the thunder roaring in the distance, farther away now.

"How do you do it?" she asked.

"Do what?"

"Live like this."

"It's not like it happens all the time," he said, trying to make it sound not as bad. "Just... whenever there is a particularly difficult case."

She wiped at her eyes. Her hair was damp and disheveled, her makeup streaked. She even looked like she'd aged a few years. "When you first told me about this, I wasn't sure what to think. As long as you were helping people, I didn't care. But..."

"Now you believe?"

"How can I not?"

Rand ground his teeth. "I'm sorry. I never meant for you to get involved."

"You weren't the one who attacked me in the bathroom."

"Yeah, but—"

"Rand. What was that thing?"

"You don't want to know."

"It picked me up and scratched me. It made me feel so bad… Like it wanted me dead."

Shindael. Hearing the desperation and sadness in her voice made him despise the demon even more. *First Georgia, now Rachel.*

"It's not something you need to worry about."

"Can you get rid of it?"

His phone vibrated in his pocket. He wondered who would call him so late at night, and then he remembered that Libby was visiting Georgia.

He fished the phone out of his jeans and checked the screen. As he thought, it was Libby. He swiped his thumb to answer.

"Rand! Watch out!"

It all happened in a split second. Rand looked up just in time to see a man run out in the middle of the road. He stopped right in front of Rand's path and held out his arms as if he were trying to catch the oncoming Jeep.

Rand slammed on the brakes and jerked the steering wheel. The car hydroplaned on the wet road and spun out of control.

They skidded in circle after circle, the smell of burning rubber filling the car and smoke swallowing the Jeep.

Rand's seatbelt latched hard into place and pinned him to the chair. He squeezed the wheel with both hands, praying they would not flip.

When they settled, he tried to relax, but his entire body was trembling and his breath came in short gasps.

"Are you okay?"

Rachel looked at him in complete terror. Fresh tears were in her eyes. "Did we…"

Did we hit him?

Rand threw off his seatbelt and opened the door. He stepped out into the rain, which quickly soaked through his jacket and jeans.

He jogged back to where the man had leapt out. But there was no sign of him at all.

He turned and saw Rachel following, arms folded across her body.

"There's no one here," Rand said.

"That's impossible," Rachel said. "He couldn't have run off that fast."

"And because of the way I swerved… I didn't have time to miss him. He should have been hit."

Rachel nodded.

Then, it occurred to Rand what had happened. "Oh."

"What?"

"He wasn't real."

Rachel eyed him, the rainwater dripping down her face. "Wasn't real?"

A loud crash came from the Jeep, startling them both.

The front driver's side tire rested on the ground, the Jeep leaning its weight into the wheel-less corner.

Rand jogged back over and found all five lug nuts

unscrewed and scattered in the puddles. "Shit," he muttered.

"How the hell did that happen?" Rachel said. But when Rand looked at her, she understood. "You mean that thing can do this kind of stuff too?"

"It can do whatever it wants, almost." Rand threw open the trunk and pulled out the jack.

"But we could have been killed!"

"I think that's the idea."

Rachel wrapped her arms around her body. Before, she had been afraid, but now Rand could tell she was also becoming angry.

Rand got down on his hands and knees and shoved the jack into place. "I'll put this back on and then drop you off."

Rachel said nothing. She only went to the passenger side, retrieved her umbrella, and opened it over Rand as he worked.

His phone rang again.

It chimed from somewhere inside the Jeep. He'd forgotten that Libby had tried to call him just before they'd spun out.

Rand straightened and found his phone underneath the car seat where it had fallen.

"Hey," he said. "Sorry about before. You're never going to believe—"

"Dad! Come to the hospital!"

He'd never heard his daughter sound so upset. "What's wrong? Are you all right?"

Rachel looked at him, concern washing over her face.

"It's Georgia! You need to get here now!"

31

R and left his Jeep at the front of St. Mary's main reception door, not caring if it got towed. He and Rachel rushed into the hospital.

The ICU was on the third floor, and the elevator opened into a large visitor waiting room. It was mostly empty at that time of night, but Libby met him there. When he saw his daughter, he could tell she'd been crying.

"Libby!" he said, running up to her. "What's wrong? What happened?"

"She just fell. Collapsed."

"What were you and her doing?"

She gave him a look. One of frozen terror.

"Libby—"

"He attacked us."

"The demon?"

"Yeah. He came for us in the hallway when we went down to get ice cream. We tried to run away, but it kept appearing in front of us. So we ran into the chapel to hide. But then he burst open the door and trashed the whole place. After, Georgia just fell down and I couldn't wake her up." Recounting the story made tears fall from her eyes again.

"Okay," Rand said, pulling her close to him. "You did well. Running for the chapel was the right thing to do."

"But it didn't work! He still hurt her. He did this to her."

"Come on. Let's go see her."

"What should I do?" Rachel asked.

"You should go," Rand told her.

"I don't want to leave you," she said. "What if the same thing happens as before? Like last time?"

Rand hated to see how worried she was for him. "It won't get the best of me again."

She nodded, but Rand could tell she wasn't so sure. Regardless, she took a seat on a couch and tried her best to calm herself.

Libby used her ICU visitor badge to scan the reader by the door to get into the ICU. But as Rand tried to follow her in, a nearby security guard placed a strong hand on his chest, holding him back. It took Rand a moment to recognize him, but finally, he did—Jerry, Harold's colleague.

"Evening, Jerry," Rand said, trying to put on his best charming smile.

"You know I can't let you in here," Jerry said quietly, looking around them. Libby stood on the other side of the ICU's threshold. "I'm supposed to call the police, but I don't want to do that, Rand. You should just leave."

"This is for Georgia," Rand said. "Please. Just give me some time."

"Harold also gave you some time, and look what

happened to him. Suspended. He's in there now, with the girl, and I wasn't even supposed to allow *that* to happen. Please, Rand. Don't put me in a tough position."

Rand met Jerry's eyes and held his ground. "I can't leave and you know that. You saw what was on those security videos. It's gotten even stronger, and now it's attacking her." Jerry let his gaze drop to the ground. "I'm the only one who can help her."

Jerry placed his hands on his hips and looked around as if checking to see if anyone was watching. "Damn it. For as much as you claim you're here to help, you sure do stir up a lot of trouble."

"My daughter and her mother would both agree with you," Rand said. "But listen. After tonight, this will be all over. Everything will go back to normal."

Jerry sighed heavily and stepped out of Rand's way.

———

THE ICU WAS A LARGE, circular room. All the patient rooms were on the periphery of the main section so that the patients could be seen at all times by the staff. Georgia was in room 316.

Inside were Nick and Maria, Father Calvin, and Harold, dressed in plain clothes.

Georgia lay on the bed, still and peaceful. Her body was straight and relaxed, arms down by her side, a thick, white blanket pulled up to her chin. She looked like she was sleeping.

She also looked dead. Rand had to tear his eyes away.

"Oh, Rand," Maria said, hugging him. "Thank you for coming."

"I drove here as soon as I could. Libby told me what happened."

Nick shook his head. "I could hardly believe it."

"The chapel is destroyed," Father Calvin said. "The girls were only in there for a few minutes while I stepped out." Calvin took out his cell phone and opened his camera roll. He showed Rand the pictures.

They weren't kidding. The entire place was ransacked and turned upside down. The stained-glass windows were smashed, the cushions in the pews were torn up, the carpet was covered with dark marks that looked like blood, and the statue of Jesus had fallen, the face broken to pieces.

"I came back to the chapel and heard screaming," Father Calvin continued. "That's where I found your daughter and Georgia. Georgia had passed out and we could not wake her up. I pressed the code-blue button on the wall, which thankfully still worked, and now we're here."

Rand looked at the girl in the bed again and ground his teeth. All of the trauma. All of the attacks. It had to end. She was too young and too sick to go through something like this. He despised the demons and how they chose their targets. They always picked on the vulnerable and unsuspecting.

"The doctors are saying coma," Nick said. "But they can't figure out why. All of her other vitals are normal."

"They don't know why she won't wake up," Maria said, wiping away a tear.

Seventeen days.

It was now the night of the sixteenth day. The demon was making good on his promise.

Rand took in a slow, deep breath. "Right. Then there is only one thing left to do."

There came a knock at the door. When Rand turned, he saw Katie slipping in, visitor badge in hand and looking worried. "How is she?"

"Coma," Nick said. "And they don't know why."

"We have to get rid of this demon," Rand told Katie. "Tonight. It attacked her and Libby, and that's why Georgia's in the coma."

And because the time limit is up.

Katie nodded. She was the only other one who knew of Georgia's ticking clock.

"Will you help?" Rand asked Calvin.

The man tensed at the suggestion, but after feeling all the eyes in the room on him, he finally said, "Whatever needs to be done for Georgia."

Rand hoped the priest would find the same courage he'd mustered for his encounter with the possessed girl all those years ago. "Do you have any holy water?"

"There are a few bottles in the chapel that weren't smashed."

"We'll need as much as you have. Can you get them now?"

Calvin nodded and left.

"Wait a minute, Rand," Katie said. "You want to do it in here? In the ICU?"

"Where else? This is where Georgia is."

"There are people around. Doctors, patients, nurses. Everyone."

"So?"

Katie looked at him incredulously. "So, it's an ICU.

You can't kick all the staff out of here. The patients are really sick."

"What other choice do we have?"

"You know how destructive this demon is," Katie went on. "There could be more damage. Vandalism. Especially when we challenge it. This is a very dangerous place for an exorcism."

She was right. But there wasn't much use in doing it in the parking lot when the demon was attached to Georgia in the ICU.

"Can we bring her to another room?" Maria asked.

"They won't let us move her when she's comatose," Nick said.

"Why not? She's our daughter. They should allow us to go anywhere we want."

"Excuse me."

The sharp voice belonged to a thin woman at the door, wearing a white coat. Her name badge read Vanessa Clarke. "There is a visitor limit in the ICU for a reason," she said, eyeing everyone in the group sternly. "There are really sick patients up here and we can't have too many people around."

"Right," Nick said. "We were just leaving, Dr. Clarke."

Dr. Clarke looked as if she didn't quite believe him, then turned and walked away.

"We'll leave you and Katie here," Nick told Rand. "And Father Calvin. You three… do what you need to do."

Rand nodded. "Sounds like a plan."

The machines attached to Georgia Collins started beeping and going haywire.

"Oh my God," Maria said.

The alarms triggered a flood of nurses into the room,

which pushed the group out like displaced water. Rand and the others waited outside 316 while Dr. Clarke rushed over and supervised the four nurses who pressed buttons on the machines, analyzed Georgia's heart rhythms, and checked her pulse and breathing.

Maria Collins started crying. Her husband pulled her close.

"She's not crashing," Rand whispered to Katie. "It's just our little friend messing with us."

The nurses who were investigating the equipment looked back at Dr. Clarke, shrugging.

"The machines aren't reading accurately," one of them said.

"Why?" Dr. Clarke asked. "What's wrong with them?" No one had an answer. "Swap them all out."

The nurses nodded and Dr. Clarke left the room, the equipment still beeping and blaring wildly behind her.

"What's going on?" Maria asked her.

"Your daughter is fine," Dr. Clarke said. "No change. The machines are reading stats that aren't correct."

Nick and Maria looked at Rand. He saw in their faces that they'd put two and two together, now silently asking him if it was the demon who was causing the malfunctions.

Dr. Clarke followed their gaze and settled her eyes on him. "There are a lot of rumors going around about Georgia Collins," she said. "Are you that man everyone's been talking about?"

"Probably."

"If I'm not mistaken, you're not allowed in this hospital anymore."

"I'm here for the same reason as you, Doctor," Rand said. "To help Georgia."

"Then why don't you leave it to the professionals?"

A loud *crack* came from Georgia's room. One machine had blown out, a rain of sparks falling onto the ground as the screen went black. The nurses all jumped back, startled. Even Dr. Clarke stared in amazement before regaining her composure.

It's escalating, Rand thought. *He's near.* He wouldn't be surprised if an apparition appeared soon. *We need to begin.* But Dr. Clarke was interfering.

"Get those things out of there!" she shouted at the nurses, and they moved double time to obey.

"Do you know why that equipment is doing that?" Rand asked. "Have you ever experienced something like that in your career?"

Dr. Clarke set her jaw and did not respond.

Father Calvin came through the ICU door, carrying a box with him. He approached the group while eyeing the chaos happening in Georgia's room. "What's going on?"

Rand ignored him for the time being. "Let me do what I need to do," he pleaded to Dr. Clarke. "What do we have to lose? You still haven't figured out what's keeping her in a coma."

"What do we have to lose?" Dr. Clarke rounded on him. "Everything! Our reputation, our accreditation, our *patients.* You threaten all of those things by being here."

"The demon doesn't care about any of that."

Dr. Clarke winced at the word. "You sound like a crazy person. I have to ask you to leave. If you don't, then I will call security." Then she walked away.

Inside Georgia's room, the nurses had powered off all

the medical equipment that surrounded her and were rolling it out.

"What are we going to do?" Katie asked.

Rand watched Dr. Clarke go. "We're not getting any support here. I think we just need to go for it." He turned to Nick and Maria Collins. "It's probably best if you two wait in the visitor area outside."

They looked at each other, frightened and hesitant to leave.

"Come on, folks," Harold said, putting his hands on their shoulders. "Let's go get some coffee."

He led them out of the ICU, Libby following close behind them. She turned and gave her dad a saddened, hopeful look.

Because they both knew if he couldn't remove the demon now, it was likely to be beyond his ability. In his past cases, Rand had been beaten, thrown around, and scratched. He'd witnessed past clients on the verge of madness, driven insane by the unexplainable terror happening around them. But in the end, he'd always won. For the first time, though, the possibility that he could be in over his head entered his mind. He remembered the morgue, and how helpless he'd been, saved only by Harold's arrival.

This one is strong, he thought. *I have to be stronger.*

There was no one else to save Georgia Collins.

"It's time," Rand said.

Calvin looked around the ICU nervously. "There are too many people and patients."

"I told him the same thing," Katie said.

"You're right," Rand said. "We need to clear them out."

"How? You can't just tell the doctor to move a bunch

of sick people out of the ward. It would take hours to relocate them safely."

"If I can't convince them, then I know what can."

It took Calvin and Katie a few moments to understand what he meant.

"No," Katie said. "Absolutely not."

Rand's idea was against his better judgment. He knew it was dangerous, and it was not something he would have normally ever done.

But he was out of options and out of time.

He went to the center of the ICU and bellowed at the top of his lungs, "Shindael!"

ll the nurses stopped short and stared at him like he was a crazy man. They weren't wrong.

"Shindael!" Rand bellowed again. "Show yourself! In the name of the Lord, I command you to come here!"

The room was silent and still, all the ambient noise created by the staff doing their jobs halting as they stopped to stare at him and look around at each other, wondering which one of them would be the first to step up and speak out.

That person was Dr. Clarke. She zipped over to him, a patient's chart in hand, glaring. "That's it. I'm calling security and the police."

Rand ignored her. "Shindael! You coward!"

"Stop screaming in here!" Dr. Clarke said through clenched teeth.

When nothing happened, Rand knew it was time to play dirty. He went to Father Calvin and grabbed a bottle of holy water from the box he still held. He bit off the cork and spat it onto the ground, then walked to the entrance of Georgia's room and tossed the water over the door in the sign of the cross. He'd learned it was sometimes better to go on the offensive. Anything holy was sure to provoke the spirit into action.

"In the name of the Lord Jesus Christ, I command you to make yourself known!"

All of the lights flickered. In response, the backup lights on the generator flared to life, and then those also lost power and went dim.

The nurses looked overhead, confused and frightened. Dr. Clarke, who had raised a phone to her ear to call security, paused and glanced around, unsure of herself.

That's it, he thought. *You hear me now.*

Rand returned to the center of the ICU and threw more holy water in the sign of the cross on the floor. "In the name of the Lord Jesus Christ, I command you to show yourself! Come out of hiding. We're here for you."

You can't disobey when commanded in the name of God.

The ICU filled with the incessant sounds of medical equipment going haywire. Beeps, alarms, and chimes all went off in every room of the ICU as if every patient had suddenly crashed at the same time.

Dr. Clarke looked around. The colored lights above each patient room flashed with an alert. "Everyone!" she called out to the frozen nurses. "Get with your patients! Close the blinds!"

The nurses moved all at once. Each one darted into a patient room, closed the door, and lowered the blinds over the windows.

The alarms dinged and the lights flickered on and off. Then, Rand experienced the unmistakable heavy feeling.

The same one from his night in the morgue when he'd encountered Shindael for the first time.

He's here. He's coming.

"Shindael!" Rand shouted again.

"What is going on?" Dr. Clarke demanded, grabbing his arm, phone and police forgotten.

"I'm saving your patient," Rand said. "That's what's going on."

Everything went silent when all the alarms stopped at the same time. The room fell into darkness, with only a few backup lights giving off a dim hue in the large room.

The temperature of the room plunged. Rand looked around, expecting Shindael to appear behind him.

And when Rand looked in front of him again, he had appeared—the boy from the morgue. The boy he'd followed around the hospital, dressed in a patient gown and holding an IV pole. He looked at the ground, his face obscured in the dim room.

Shindael disguised as Thomas.

"Does everyone see him?" Rand whispered.

No one around him said anything. They only nodded. Katie, Calvin, Dr. Clarke. Shindael had materialized for all of them. He stood only a few steps away.

Which meant he was done hiding. He was ready to fight.

And so was Rand.

"Shindael. Your time here is finished. We don't want you here anymore, and you need to leave."

The boy looked up at him, a knowing smirk on his face. His eyes were only two pools of black that Rand could not bear to look into.

"In the name of Jesus Christ, I command you to leave," Rand shouted at him.

The boy glowered. "No!"

The voice that came from him was deep and rough, not human. Rand's entire body tensed, remembering the morgue and what the entity was capable of.

"You must do what I command of you in the name of the Lord. You are powerless against God."

"Bullshit!" he shot back.

"Our Father, who art in heaven," Father Calvin prayed, "hallowed be thy name."

When removing a demonic presence, it was a good approach to have at least one person pray unceasingly. Invoking the presence of the Lord was a powerful strategy.

"Shut up, old man!"

"That's enough, Shindael!" Rand shouted. He raised the bottle of holy water and cast it toward the demon. When it landed on Shindael, he acted as if it was acid searing into him, crying out in pain.

Then, the boy changed.

His body grew into a terrible being that stood twice the size of Rand. His head almost reached the ceiling. The face changed from that of a human to one that resembled a bat, its mouth filled with razor-sharp teeth. His ears became pointed and his skin was black and scaly.

The body morphed into some sort of reptile. Skinny arms, bent at the elbows, and disproportionally large hands with three sharp claws at the end.

The eyes were completely black.

Rand's body told him to take a step back, told him that

this creature was large enough to bite him in half and destroy the entire hospital.

"And lead us not into temptation, but deliver us from evil," Calvin continued to pray. Tears streaked his cheeks as he forced himself to look at the demon—forced himself to remain faithful.

Although it was terrible to look at, Rand knew this was progress. He had gotten it to reveal its true form. No more disguises. He looked upon the real Shindael for the first time, and while his heart pounded in his chest—while his legs ached to run—he stood his ground, facing down this powerful being.

So, this is you, he thought. *So large and evil, targeting a girl as young as Georgia.*

As Calvin continued to pray, Rand did not let up on his commands. "In the name of Jesus Christ, I command you to leave this place!"

Again he threw holy water onto the demon, making the sign of the cross. It stumbled back, angry and sneering, acting as if it was burned by the fluid.

Rand pushed forward. "In the name of Jesus Christ, I command you to leave this place!"

Shindael shouted something back at him, but Rand could not understand. Ancient Sumerian, he assumed.

"You are not welcome here, demon," Rand said. "Return to hell where you belong." Rand used his hands to trace out the sign of the cross in the air, forming a barrier between him and the demon. "And we will hear from you no more. You will leave this place alone, and you will not torment the patients anymore. You will free the spirits of the children you have held here, and they will move on to the afterlife. Then, you will return to hell."

Shindael roared at him one last time as Rand used the rest of the holy water. "Leave now! In the name of Jesus Christ, *leave this place once and for all!*"

Shindael fell to his knees as if punctured and deflating. Then his body morphed into a large cloud of black smoke and seemed to disintegrate into thin air.

The room fell silent. The only sound was Rand's heart pounding in his ears.

After a few long moments, he let out the breath he'd been holding. *He's gone. Sent away. It's over.*

The lights of the ICU returned to normal. The temperature rose, melting away the icy chill the demon had brought along with it.

Rand looked around the room, searching for any trace of the lingering demonic spirit. *You're safe now, Georgia.*

"Amen," Father Calvin said behind him.

ONCE THE PLACE WAS QUIET, the nurses came out from where they had holed themselves up in the patient rooms.

Katie gripped Rand's arm.

"Rand."

When he saw the look on her face, he frowned. "What's wrong?"

"He's still here."

"What? How can that be? We saw him leave."

The apparition, then the dematerializing, then the vanishing. It was all by the book. That's what happened every time he'd successfully banished the demonic.

"I don't know, but something is off." She looked

around the room as if waiting for the silence to speak to her. Her brow furrowed. "Something's wrong."

"Are you sure?"

"I always get that clear, pure feeling after we remove an entity from a place. I don't have that now. In fact, it keeps getting worse." Her face twisted as if the feeling was weighing down on her painfully. "Rand, we missed something—"

And then he heard a voice from inside Georgia's room. *"Randolph Casey!"*

Through the glass windows that looked into her room, they all watched as comatose Georgia Collins shot up straight in bed.

And turned her head toward them.

Her eyes were completely black, and she smiled a sharp-toothed grin that sent chills down Rand's spine.

33

She's possessed.

The final stage of any demonic encounter. Once inside her body, the demon could control her and cause serious harm.

"We need to restrain her!" Rand grabbed the nearest nurse and pushed him into Georgia's room. The nurse resisted, afraid, but Rand forced him. "Now!"

A possessed person was completely controlled by the entity inside them, so it was paramount that they be tied down.

The nurse found the patient restraints at the bottom of the hospital bed and deftly wrapped the first around Georgia's left wrist. Rand watched him and started to do the same on her right, but Georgia yanked her arm away. Rand pulled it back, trying to slip the restraint onto her wrist. Georgia snapped her teeth at his hand, trying to bite him. The nurse helped straighten Georgia's arm and they managed to tie her wrist, then fastened the restraints together below the bed.

Her body writhed and her wrists pulled against the restraints, while she glared at the nurse with her black eyes. "Let me go!" she spat with a dark voice that was not her own. The nurse froze in terror, then turned and fled.

Her face was scaly, ears pointed, taking on some of Shindael's features.

Rand took a step back and looked at the girl. The demon turned his attention to him, staring at him through Georgia's body.

He has her now. I thought he was gone, but...

Possession was a demon's ultimate goal. Georgia being in a coma was the perfect opportunity. She had no control. No willpower or mindfulness to defend against it.

That was why he put her in a coma in the chapel. To prepare her for this.

Rand stared at her, helpless and crushed. He thought he'd won, but actually—

"You've lost, Randolph," Shindael told him, his voice an unnerving mix between his own and Georgia's. "The girl is mine, just like she was always meant to be."

Not yet. I can get her back. "We'll see about that, you son of a bitch."

Shindael only grinned at him.

Rand went outside of Georgia's room and closed the door, isolating the demon from the rest of the ward.

Katie looked ill. Calvin stared through the glass at the girl, face fallen. Tears leaked from the corners of his eyes. Rand felt exactly the same, but he'd run out of tears for these situations long ago.

"What is going on in here?"

Fiona Shaw stormed in and her stony gaze came to rest on Rand. "How did I know you'd be here?" She crossed her arms over her chest, rubbing them with her hands, shivering.

"You knew it was me because you know what's going on in this hospital," Rand said.

"Please listen to him, Miss Shaw," Calvin said. "It's serious, and it's real."

"Enough," Fiona spat at him. "I'm surprised at you, Father, that you would allow—"

"Randolph!" the demon's horrible voice pierced through the walls.

Fiona stared at the door of 316. "Who was that?" When she went to open the door, Calvin went to stop her, but Rand only held him back.

Fiona threw open the door to Georgia's room. Shindael growled at her through Georgia's body, his sharp-toothed mouth open wide.

Fiona immediately slammed the door back into place, trembling. All color had drained from her skin.

"W-w-what..."

"He's possessed her," Rand said. "And now we need to exorcise."

"What did I just see?" Fiona asked him. Her eyes began to fill with tears.

"You know what you saw," Rand said. "Now please let us do our job."

Fiona only brought her hands to her face, looking away from him. Unable to say anything else.

"This is the strongest entity I've ever faced, for sure," Rand told her. "We chased him from this room, and so he went inside Georgia. She was susceptible because of the coma. But if we can expel him from her body, he'll have nowhere left to go."

Calvin swallowed heavily and nodded, crossing himself.

An ear-splitting roar sounded through the ward.

"RANDOLPH!"

Shindael's voice pierced them like knives, the sound waves reverberating like they came through a hundred amplifiers. The glass in the windows of all the patient rooms shook, and then shattered, bursting into a cloud of shards. Ceiling tiles came loose and fell to the ground. Rand and the others dropped low, hands over their heads as the debris crashed down.

When everything had fallen, the only sound in the ward was Shindael's gleeful laughter.

They stood. Tears now streamed down Fiona's face. "What is going on? I've never seen anything—"

Rand grabbed Fiona by the shoulder. "I can save her. You just have to trust me. Evacuate the ICU. All of the patients. It's not safe as long as the demon's still here."

She stared at him for a few moments, seeming to not comprehend. Then, she slowly nodded and pulled out her cell phone.

RAND PACED NERVOUSLY BACK and forth in the main room of the ICU, crucifix in one hand and cell phone in the other. The broken shards of glass and debris from the ceiling crunched underneath his shoes. He sent a message to Miller Landingham:

Head bat, body dragon.

Knowing a demon's appearance was always helpful. Hopefully, the man could dig up some more information on Shindael. Maybe give them a reason for why they were making no progress in banishing him. At that point, anything would be helpful.

Then Rand started praying.

"God, please be with me now. Give me the strength to cast out this demon."

Father Calvin did the same. Rand noticed that the man could not stop trembling. That was normal, and Rand felt for the man. *Time to face your fears. Time to reconcile what happened to you twenty years ago.*

Patient transporters had arrived and systematically worked to roll the ICU patients from their destroyed rooms. Some of the patients were conscious while others were not, on ventilators that breathed for them, oblivious to all that was going on around them. Fiona Shaw supervised the movement while Dr. Clarke inspected each patient on his or her way out the door.

The blinds in Georgia's room were pulled down, but since the windows were broken, they could clearly hear Shindael's voice.

"You've already lost, Randolph. Ha ha ha." A patient was pushed by Georgia's room. "Oh, there goes Mr. Gilbert. He's not going to make it. So sad."

"Go," Fiona told the transporter, and ushered him out the door.

The demon rambled on, talking to himself, taking pleasure in the sound of his own voice. "Randolph Casey, I thought I called for you." More laughter. "Do you want to fuck little Georgia? I promise I'll lie still for you. Ha ha ha."

Trying to get a rise out of me, Rand thought. It was a classic ploy. *Not going to work.*

Calvin approached Rand. "Are you ready?"

"Yes. How about you?"

Calvin did not answer.

"You need faith," Rand told him. "Be strong. You've done this before. And you were successful last time."

Calvin looked down at his feet. "You're right. For Georgia."

"The patients are all gone," Fiona said, coming up to Rand. Harold was with her.

"Good." Then, to Harold, he said, "How are Nick and Maria?"

"Worried," he said. "Far worse than that, actually. They heard all the commotion."

"Do they know that Georgia…"

"No. Of course not."

"Stay with them, please."

Harold nodded.

"Will you three be all right in here alone?" Fiona asked.

"Yes. Now go with Harold. The next time you see us, this place will be back to normal again."

Rand could tell Fiona wanted to believe that but was unsure. She and Harold left, and Rand, Katie, and Calvin were the only ones who remained in the deserted, destroyed ICU.

"I'm getting lonely in here," came the voice. "Won't someone come and play with me?"

This was it. If Rand couldn't cast the demon out now, then he'd lose her for good.

"Let's kick this bastard out of here," Rand said.

34

Miller Landingham sat on a folding chair in his back office at the bookstore, flipping channels with the remote in one hand and his take-out noodles in the other. He slurped down another pile as he thumbed the channel button.

Soon, if things kept going the way they were, he'd have to cancel the cable to the store. It was probably something he should have done a while ago, but he loved television. Strange for someone who owned and operated a used bookstore.

He passed by the news, which was on the screen just long enough for him to see BREAKING on the bottom ticker. He went back up.

The reporter stood in front of St. Mary's. It was being evacuated.

That's where that little girl stays. The one Rand was taking care of.

"A couple dozen ICU patients are being transferred to a nearby facility," the woman was saying.

"And is there any more word on the problem?" asked the man in the studio on the other half of the split screen.

"All we could get was 'a widespread electrical malfunction.' We assume it's serious enough to threaten the safety of the patients."

Behind the reporter, several ambulances and police cars were parked with their lights on.

In his gut, Miller knew this had something to do with his buddy Randolph.

"All right," said the man on the television. "Keep us updated as the story develops."

The female reporter disappeared off the screen as the man started talking about a celebrity scandal.

Miller's phone beeped with a text from Rand.

Head bat, body dragon.

So Rand had finally gotten a clear glimpse of what he was dealing with.

Miller knew what it meant. In their natural form, demons often resembled combinations of real-world animals.

Noodles forgotten, Miller went to his computer and opened the database he'd been building for years.

Head of a bat, body of a dragon.

Rand had mentioned the name Shindael. Miller had found a few stories from those who had encountered Shindael, but none of them had ever described his appearance.

Miller ran a search for bat and dragon. A few possible candidates showed up. None of whom were named Shindael.

"It isn't him," Miller muttered to himself.

He searched again.

Head of bat. Body of dragon. Sick people.

It turned up nothing. He had no information on a demon of that description who particularly enjoyed preying on sick people.

"We've received word that upwards of thirty patients have been evacuated," the voice on the TV said behind him. "If you're just joining us for this breaking story, a widespread electrical malfunction at St. Mary's Medical Center has forced the evacuation of their ICU."

"St. Mary's..." Miller said to himself, remembering what Rand had told him about there being hundreds of children's spirits trapped in the ward there. He typed in a new search.

Head of bat. Body of dragon. Children.

This time he had one result.

It was a story from an internet forum he'd copied and pasted many years ago, but one he had no recollection of. It was a long block of text recounting the writer's experience with a supernatural haunting in a home they'd just moved into.

Allegedly, they'd purchased the house in 1985 for a bargain. Once there, they'd experienced the usual occurrences that Miller was used to reading about. Missing valuables, strange bumps in the night, cold spots, feelings of dread when in certain rooms.

Then, the writer's children complained of a monster that lived in their closet. At first, the writer explained, he thought it was just his kid having normal fears. But then the writer began catching glimpses of the creature in the periphery of his vision.

When he looked into it, he discovered that the house had been built on the site of a tragedy ten years before. A preschool had burned down, and thirteen children had perished in the fire.

Miller leaned in close to his computer screen as he read, feeling he was on to something. *Burned down preschool.*

The writer explained that he'd brought in a priest to bless the home and remove the negative energy, and whatever was living there had fought back. He saw it for the first time and wrote that it looked like a mixture between a bat and a dragon or lizard. Maybe a dinosaur.

The priest had commanded the entity to reveal its name, which he said was Karax. He used the name to send the demon away, and for a few weeks it seemed to have worked, and there was peace again. But then the strange occurrences happened again. The family eventually had to move out of the house.

Miller leaned back in his chair. This was why he farmed the internet daily for people's accounts of their hauntings and kept a record of them. With enough shared information, cross-references were possible.

Karax, Miller thought. He ran a search for the name, but still, the only result was the story he'd already read.

The physical description and the habit of going after children were two identifying factors that were too strong to pass up.

Miller picked up his phone and tried to call Rand. It went straight to voicemail.

"Come on, pick up," he muttered as he tried once more. Since the ICU had to be evacuated, he knew his friend was probably in the middle of an all-out battle.

But he needed to get through. Rand was using the wrong name.

The demon meant to fool you, and it worked.

35

Rand led the way into the room, pushing open the door and going to stand at the foot of the bed. Calvin was behind his right shoulder, Katie at his left.

Georgia looked even more like the demon. Her hair had changed from blonde to white and the flesh over her entire body had turned scaly and reptilian.

Shindael gave his fanged grin. "Oh. Is it time?" Father Calvin was the first to move. He held his Bible out toward the demon, who recoiled from it, the grin replaced by a glaring scowl. "Fuck off!"

"Lord in heaven," Calvin said, continuing his bombardment of prayer, "deliver Georgia Collins from this servant of evil. Reclaim her for your kingdom and expel this wretched creature from inside her."

"Not going to work, Father!" Shindael spat at him, although Rand could see that the prayers still pained him.

"Shindael, I command you by name," Rand said. "Depart from the body of this girl."

Shindael turned his attention to Rand. "Who the fuck is Shindael? Ha ha ha."

"You are. You are a liar and a coward and a monster, and you must do what I command of you."

"*I* command you to fuck this priest!" Shindael threw his head back and roared in laughter.

Rand had heard all the clever comebacks before. He held the crucifix out, which instantly made Shindael cease his laughing. He stared at it as if waiting for Rand to plunge it into his heart.

"Yeah, you know what this is," Rand said. "And you know what it means. It has power over you."

Shindael regarded the cross for a few moments before turning to Katie, acknowledging her presence for the first time. "Aren't you pretty," he muttered.

Rand knew what was happening. When faced with something that made him feel threatened, a demon would always try to exploit some other weakness in the room. Demons he'd faced in the past usually assumed Katie would be the weakest among them.

Katie did not flinch when the black eyes landed on her. "I'm not afraid of you," she said, not a hint of fear in her voice.

"Maybe not," Shindael said. "But they are." He nodded his head, gesturing past Father Calvin and out into the hall.

Katie looked and froze. Rand had seen that look before. He followed Katie's gaze out to the main section of the ICU and found nothing. But he already knew what she saw.

The other children. Shindael knows they affect her.

"Yes, you see them now, don't you? I called them here.

They do whatever I say. They are my slaves."

"They're here," Katie whispered. "All those kids."

"I collect them," Shindael said. "They die, and I capture their souls. They belong to me because they're weak and stupid." He laughed again.

A sudden fury coursed through Rand, reminded that Georgia was not the only one at stake.

He's trying to make us angry. Provoke us.

He held the cross out toward Shindael again. He stepped around to the side of the bed, bringing the crucifix closer. Shindael recoiled away, not wanting to be burned. Rand gripped it, knuckles turning white. Anger flared through him at the thought of all the children who had not been allowed to move on because of this creature. "In the name of the Lord Jesus Christ, I command you to leave this place and free these spirits from your hold."

"No! They're mine!"

"They do not belong to you. They belong to God."

"Then tell him to come and get them!"

Shindael turned toward Father Calvin, who had been praying ceaselessly since he'd begun. "The forces of hell are of no match for you, Lord, and we have faith that you will intervene and protect us from this evil."

"Shut up, old man!" Shindael shouted. "I've heard enough out of you!"

"This demon, Shindael, is a servant of Lucifer, and has no power here where your Kingdom reigns."

"You'll hang yourself after this," Shindael said. "You'll finish what you started twenty-five years ago. Because you are weak and pathetic, and your God knows it too!"

Calvin's prayer hit a sharp bump.

"Don't listen to him," Rand said.

"Little Betty. You remember her, don't you? She was never the same after that night. She's dead now, you know. No, you *don't* know, because you never cared about her. Only about yourself!"

"Lord, please—"

"Enough of that. Where was your God when you last did this? Where was he when you wanted to kill yourself? Where was he when he let Betty get taken?" Shindael laughed. "Not there. He doesn't care about you. You remember my friend Ezu, don't you?"

At the mention of the name, Father Calvin ceased praying. *Ezu.* Rand figured that was the demon who'd Calvin had encountered before.

"Yes, you do remember. And he remembers you very well."

"You're a liar," Calvin said, voice trembling.

"Am I? Come with me to hell. You can meet Betty and Ezu and be one big happy family."

"That's enough," Rand said. If he let Shindael go on about Calvin's past, he knew they'd lose ground.

But Shindael only looked to Katie, fixing her in his cold glare. His dried and broken lips spread into a menacing grin. "And what are you doing here? Did your old boyfriend drag you into this?" He chuckled.

"I won't listen to you," Katie said.

"Did you ever tell him the truth?"

Katie's mouth pressed into a thin line. "There is no truth that could ever come from you."

"Fine. Be selfish. Don't tell him about your miscarriage."

Katie's entire body tensed.

"Why haven't you told him? Don't you think Daddy

deserves to know?"

"Stop it!" Katie shrieked. But Shindael only laughed.

Miscarriage? She was pregnant?

"Oh yes. It was yours, Randolph, and she never told you," Shindael said, as if reading his thoughts. "Then she lost it. Now that baby is down in hell with me. I know because I've seen it. A little boy."

When Rand looked at Katie, he saw the brokenness in her eyes. The guilt was clear on her face, and Rand knew that everything Shindael had said was true.

The memories came flooding back to him. The abrupt end of their relationship. She'd called it off with no explanation, disappeared, and stopped returning his calls. Then when he'd finally gotten in touch with her months later, she'd told him she could no longer work as a medium.

His own tears formed in the corners of his eyes. Pictures of him with a son, a baby brother for Libby, flashed through his mind. A future that was possible, but he'd never known. *Because she kept it from me.*

"Rand, I'm so sorry," Katie said through her sobs.

Seeing her despair snapped him back into the moment. He saw what Shindael was trying to do. Anger coursed through him so strongly and so suddenly that Rand shoved the crucifix onto Shindael's forehead. It sizzled like raw meat on a frying pan, and Shindael wailed in pain. Smoke billowed from the spot where the wood pressed into his skin.

"In the name of Jesus Christ," Rand said through gritted teeth, into the demon's ear, "I command you, Shindael, evil spirit, to leave this girl forever. Go back to hell."

"Fuck you!" Shindael shouted through his cries.

Rand pulled the cross away. It left a red mark on the black, scaly skin.

Shindael recovered from the pain of the burn and glared at him. "Give it up, Randolph. It isn't going to work. This is the end of the road for you."

Georgia's body looked less and less like herself as the demon spent more time inside her, taking over.

He's right. It's not working. This bastard isn't budging.

Rand caught the negative thoughts in his head and pushed them away, hopefully before Shindael could sense that he was having them.

"Rand…" Calvin said.

Rand could see that Calvin was thinking the same thing. Nothing was working. They needed a new approach. A new idea.

Then Katie fled from the room, crying, the trauma of her secret being exposed getting the best of her.

My team is falling apart, Rand realized.

Shindael only chuckled. "You're a failure, Randolph. Now, can you untie me so I can play with myself before I kill the girl? Ha ha."

Ignoring him, Rand left the room, pulling Calvin along with him to the main section of the ICU. The lights were out now, leaving them in a shroud of darkness.

"Rand," Katie said.

"It's okay," he said, though he wasn't sure just how okay it really was. *It has to be. We cannot change it. Shindael wants us to get emotional.*

"I'm so sorry," she said. "I didn't know what to do. It was years ago. I was—"

"You don't need to explain," Rand told her gently. "We can talk about that later."

"Nothing we do is working," Calvin said. "Shindael seems immune to all prayers. He won't budge."

"He's very strong," Rand said, keeping his voice low, not wanting Shindael to overhear.

"We must be missing something," Calvin said.

Rand scratched at his chin. The priest was correct. The demon was showing a huge amount of resilience, a level that Rand had never encountered before.

I can't let the self-doubt into my head.

Because once that slippery slope began, there was nothing left but a glide to the bottom. Then, he might never get Georgia Collins back.

Miller, he remembered suddenly.

He fished his phone from his pocket and saw a bunch of missed calls from Miller.

Odd. He hadn't felt it vibrate. His phone must have been messed up along with all the other electrical equipment in the ICU.

Rand tapped the screen and called him back.

"Who are you calling?" Calvin asked.

Miller answered on the first ring. "Rando! Thank God!"

"Is everything all right?"

"You tell me. You're doing an exorcism at St. Mary's, aren't you?"

"Yeah. How did you—"

"They've evacuated and it's all over the news."

"We're dealing with a full-on possession now," Rand told him. "He's so strong. Nothing seems to—"

"Rand, it's not Shindael." Miller spoke fast and breathlessly as if he'd just run a mile.

Rand turned to face the other two. "What?"

"It's what I've been trying to call you about. That demon is *not* Shindael."

Rand paused for a moment. "How do you know?"

"I searched the description you sent me. A cross between a bat and a dragon. Bat head, dragon body."

"That's it," Rand said.

"His real name is Karax. He's a known servant of Shindael, one of hundreds. And he likes to hurt children. I found a story of another priest who encountered him at the site of a preschool that burned down a decade ago."

That bastard, Rand thought. *He gave me the wrong name.*

"It's the only thing that makes sense," Miller said. "Why would he have given you his name? Because it's the *wrong* one. He gave you his master's name, not his own. So if you've been trying to command him to leave by invoking the wrong name, then you're not using your full authority."

"Karax," Rand said, the word tasting like poison on his lips. Calvin and Katie exchanged an uneasy glance.

"That's it," Miller said. "Next time you face him, try commanding him with his real name."

"All right, I'm going back in there."

"Good luck, Rando. Be careful. Have faith."

Rand hung up and glared at the door of room 316. The blinds were drawn, but he could still hear the demon muttering to himself.

"Who was that?" Calvin asked.

Rand stormed over, crucifix gripped in his hand.

"Rand!"

"You two wait out here." He knew his anger was getting the best of him, that he should not face down this creature alone. But Karax had already gotten into their heads and thrown them off.

Rand stepped through the door and threw aside the curtain.

"Welcome back," the demon said, grinning at him, an evil mirth in his blackened eyes. "Are you here to untie me now?"

"I don't believe we've ever met before, Karax."

And for the first time, the smile faded from the demon's lips.

36

His eyes bored into Rand and a low growl rumbled from the back of his throat.

"Karax," Rand repeated.

"Don't say that!" he snapped.

"Why not?"

"Because—"

"Why don't you want me to say it, Karax?"

"Fuck you! Eat shit!"

"Not today, Karax." Rand walked around to the side of the bed, getting closer to Karax, who, for the first time, looked afraid in his presence. His black eyes went to the cross in Rand's hand. "This is over."

"You're right," Karax said, his voice low and dark. "I'm done. But I'll take the girl with me. I can stop her heart whenever I want. I'm inside her, remember? And it'll be all your fault that she died."

Now that Rand knew Karax's name, the demon was running out of defenses. He had to end this now, or it would be too late.

Rand held up the crucifix and Karax recoiled. "In the name of the Lord Jesus Christ, I command you, Karax, to leave the body of this girl."

Karax had nothing to say in return. He trembled underneath the presence of the cross.

Rand reached for the nearby box Calvin had brought from the chapel. He took a bottle of holy water and yanked the cork out with his teeth.

"No," Karax said. "Look at the door!"

Rand ignored him, figuring Karax was only trying to distract him. But then movement at the entrance of the room caught his eye.

Oh my God...

The ghostly apparitions of children filled the room like a solemn procession. Their bodies were a soft blue light, half transparent, their expressions hollow and empty. They seemed to glide through the air rather than walk. They surrounded Rand and the bed, crowding him.

Some were tall, others were short. Some looked to be about fifteen, while others were as young as four or five. Some wore hospital gowns, and some wore clothes from the '70s and the '80s, as well as the present day.

Rand had never seen so many apparitions at once. They all seemed so lost and hopeless.

There are hundreds of children here, Katie had said. Now he fully understood why she had been so upset that night.

"All of them are mine," Karax said, grinning again. "Some have been here for decades."

The faces of even more apparitions peered at him through the window outside the room. All looked longingly at him, as if desperate for his help.

They are, Rand thought. *I'm their only chance of moving on.*

Rand tore his eyes from those of the ghostly children and glared at Karax. "You will free these souls. They belong to God."

"Wrong again!" Karax shouted. "They stay because God does not want them. Ha ha!"

Rand threw the holy water at Karax in the sign of the cross. Georgia's body trembled and writhed under the fiery pain.

"I can go inside you next!" Karax's voice was now high and shrill, a desperate scream. "I'll make you a pedophile! I've done it so many times before. It's too easy!"

Rand knew it was an empty threat. Karax was finally feeling cornered.

"In the name of the Lord Jesus Christ, I command you to let these children go and to leave the body of this girl!"

Rand threw the holy water again. He touched the cross to Georgia's heart, and the demon convulsed underneath it.

"Take it away! Make it stop!"

"You know what you have to do if you want it to stop," Rand said.

"Fine! Fine!"

"Do it, Karax."

And then the apparitions of the children around Rand turned into balls of blue light, little orbs that hovered in the air. They lingered there for a moment before blinking out like a flipped light switch.

They're moving on.

They disappeared one by one until they were all gone.

"There!" Karax shouted.

"And now you," Rand said, the crucifix continuing to burn the demon. "Leave here now, and your pain will end."

Karax, amidst his bellowing, found new strength and broke the restraint on his right wrist. He swatted the cross from Rand's hand and it clattered to the floor on the other side of the room.

Karax used his free hand to tear the other restraint, and in an instant, he was loose.

No!

"Take them all," Karax said, his voice low and grumbling. He glared at Rand through his black eyes. "I don't need them anymore. But the girl is mine. Her time is up."

Rand's mouth went dry.

"That's right," Karax went on. "You know what I mean. Seventeen days. Why do you care so much, Randolph? No matter what you do, the girl will die anyway."

"That's not true," Rand said, although he knew it could be. When he'd first heard Karax on the recording, there had been no way to know if he'd meant Georgia would die from cystic fibrosis or be killed by him in seventeen days' time.

And he still didn't know.

Karax must've seen his thoughts on his face. "You don't know. You can't know. But I do, and I'm not going to tell you. All of this could be for nothing." He smirked.

Karax leapt upright on the bed, lithe and nimble like an acrobat, then jumped through the air, landed, and ran with blinding speed out of the ICU.

37

Rand grabbed the crucifix from where it had fallen onto the floor and took off after the demon. He only caught a glimpse of Karax fleeing before the demon bounded through the main doors of the ICU.

Rand sprinted after Karax. The situation was bad enough, but having a demon-possessed girl running loose through the halls of the hospital was far more dangerous than anything else. Karax had all but destroyed the ICU, and he could easily extend that havoc to the rest of the hospital.

In the hallway, Rand's eyes darted from side to side. He spotted the door to the stairwell falling closed. When he burst through, he found Karax crouching on the steps leading up.

"Give it up, Randolph!"

Rand ran up the stairs, but Karax only leapt away from him, clearing entire floors with a single jump. Rand had to take three steps at a time just to keep up.

"You can't have her!" the demon's voice echoed down to him through the stairwell.

You're wrong about that.

Rand rounded a corner on level 15R and saw the door falling closed. He followed Karax through it and found himself in a hallway that looked like it was under construction. Definitely not the main part of the hospital.

It was a long corridor with plywood for walls. At the end, near a set of double doors, a security guard crouched by the wall, eyes wide and trembling.

"Where is she?" Rand asked the man.

"W-w-what was that thing?"

"Where did she go?"

The guard lifted a shaky finger and pointed to the doors on Rand's left. Then he rose to his feet and ran away in terror.

Rand pushed through the doors and stopped short. He was outside, the cool air and heavy wind slapping him hard in the face. The rest of St. Mary's upper floors loomed above him. Red lights flashed in a circle on the ground.

The hospital helipad.

He spotted Karax on the far end of the helipad, standing right on the edge. The wind whipped at Georgia's whitened hair and hospital gown, so strong it should have blown her over the side. Only the demon kept her footing sure.

He means to throw her off. That's how he wants to finish her.

Rand and Karax eyed each other from opposite ends of the roof. He was maybe thirty paces away from Georgia. But the landing pad was wide between them, seeming miles in that moment.

Rand ventured a step forward, hoping Karax would not drop himself off.

The demon did not move. So Rand pressed on, crucifix gripped by his side.

When he was halfway there, Karax finally spoke. "This place was special to her. There's no better location for her to die." He smiled.

Proud of your own theatrics, Rand thought. He stopped advancing, letting the standoff continue.

"Since you care so much about her, I assume you'd like to share her fate," Karax went on. "You can lead the way down!"

Karax broke into an inhumanly fast sprint, closing the distance between them in milliseconds. He pounced on Rand, knocking him backward and wrestling him to the ground with ease. The crucifix spun away and out of reach.

Hands went to Rand's face, jagged thumbs aimed at his eyes. Georgia's fingers had elongated, topped by long, yellow fingernails. Rand caught his wrists just in time and fought back against them, but the demon was lending Georgia's body powerful strength.

"The girl dies tonight," Karax growled at him. "And I'll take you with me. All three of us in hell together!"

Karax leapt off of him and broke free of his grasp. He gripped Rand by the front of his shirt and pulled him to his feet, the seams ripping as he did. Rand tried to resist, but the demon dragged him to the edge of the helipad, slung him around, and pressed his back against nothing but the empty air. The wind whipped at him, and the lights from the police cars and ambulances that had arrived to evacuate the patients flashed what seemed like miles beneath him.

Rand held onto Karax's wrists, but the demon could let him topple over the side whenever he wanted.

He's so strong. So quick.

Rand had never encountered anything like it before. No matter what he did, he always seemed to be at Karax's mercy.

Karax's black eyes bored into him, studying him. Then his lips parted into a sharp-toothed smile. "Shindael will be pleased I brought you down with me."

Karax released him, and Rand toppled backward. His entire body felt like one of those dreams where he was falling, only to wake up at the last minute.

Just before he fell out of reach, Karax caught him again, pulling him back to the edge. It was the closest to death Rand had ever been, and his body knew it. Everything felt numb as if it had all shut down to accept it.

Karax squealed with laughter. "You should see your face!"

A sound from overhead.

A helicopter lowered over the landing pad, stirring up a heavy wind that ripped at Rand's clothes and Georgia's hospital gown.

The demon twisted its head to look at it. The white, stringy hair blew in the gusts from the spinning blades.

One last chance. Rand had only a moment while Karax was distracted. He slipped his hand into his jacket pocket and gripped the last vial of holy water.

Karax looked back at him just in time for Rand to

smash the vial onto his scaly face. The glass broke, the shards stabbing into Rand's palm.

Smoke erupted from Karax's forehead where the bottle had broken. Rand pushed forward at that moment, the momentum knocking Karax off his feet while he screamed in agony.

Rand dragged him back to the center of the helipad, the whipping sounds of the chopper blades drowning all the cries of the demon.

"Clear the helipad for landing!" Someone was dangling out the door of the helicopter, a megaphone up to their mouth. The chopper hovered in the air above them, stuck in limbo.

Working on it, Rand thought.

Rand threw Karax down onto his back in the center of the helipad. Rand's bloody palm stained the front of the hospital gown. He picked up the crucifix and pressed it to Karax's forehead. It burned and sizzled like the holy water.

Rand brought his face close to Karax's so the demon could hear him over the sound of the chopper blades. "In the name of the Lord Jesus Christ, I command you to leave the body of this girl!"

Rand moved the cross to Karax's chest and his body convulsed. "You have no place here anymore! Leave this girl's body and never return. Karax, the Lord commands you by name to *depart from this place.*"

Karax's scream erupted like a volcano, a deafening shout that threatened to blow out Rand's hearing. Every instinct of his wanted to curl into a ball on the ground and guard his ears from that horrible sound.

But he stayed firm. Held the cross to Georgia's chest. Watched as Karax threw his head back, eyes clenched, bellowing.

It's finally working.

And then a black mass of smoke spewed from Georgia's mouth, like a cloud of evil that seeped from her insides. It rose into the air, formless and dark, and then scattered as if a wind had carried it away.

Rand knew that sight well. It meant victory. *He's gone.*

Georgia's body lost all tension. The scaly skin softened into pale flesh. Her white hair changed back to the blonde curls. Her face relaxed and became peaceful. The transformation reversed right in front of Rand's eyes.

Yes. Come back to us, Georgia.

"Clear the helipad immediately!" the man shouted from above.

In the final moments of his fight, Rand had completely forgotten they were about to be crushed by a landing helicopter. He scooped Georgia up, arms under her neck and knees, then carried her inside as the helicopter landed behind him, the powerful gusts threatening to topple him over.

He placed her on the floor, where she opened her eyes and stirred awake.

"Georgia?"

"Where am I?" She blinked a few times and looked at him. It took a few moments before recognition dawned on her face. "Ghost Man?"

Rand broke into a smile. "Yes. It's me."

Georgia pushed herself to a sitting position, and Rand supported her back with his hand. She was weak and wobbly but managed to find some strength.

"How do you feel?" Rand asked.

She assessed herself briefly, and then said, "I'm starving. I want a cheeseburger."

38

Ten minutes later, Nick and Maria reunited with their daughter in the ICU. A quick assessment by Dr. Clarke and a team of nurses determined that nothing was wrong with Georgia. Her cystic fibrosis remained, but the coma had come and gone with no rational explanation. At least, not one that modern medicine could provide.

Rand stood outside her hospital room and watched through the broken windows. The family sat together on Georgia's bed. Rand knew from experience that Georgia would have no recollection of her possession. No one ever did. That, in itself, was a blessing.

Maintenance crews had appeared to clean up the glass and plaster that covered the floor. A second team brought ladders to replace and repair the blown-out light fixtures overhead.

Fiona Shaw oversaw the restoration, eyeing the patients as they passed her by, asking the maintenance men about the severity of the damage and how long it would take to fix. Once, she caught Rand's gaze, and she nodded. Rand thought he saw just the hint of a smile on her thin, tight lips. And he figured that meant *thank you*. It was good enough for him.

Rand slung his bag over his shoulder and walked toward the exit of the ICU, feeling like he was in the way as everyone around him worked to put the place back together. He considered stepping into room 316, but he stopped short and lingered on the threshold. The family huddled close, Nick and Maria sitting on Georgia's bed, and they talked low amongst themselves. Maria cradled her daughter against her chest. None of them noticed him there. So, without saying a word, he left them to be with each other.

He already knew the next twenty-four hours would be the hardest of anything so far—at least for him. It would be nothing but waiting. Karax was gone, but the demon's original threat still remained. *Seventeen days.* The prediction could still come true. After everything, they could still lose Georgia to her disease.

All Rand could do was pray and hope.

In the hallway outside, Father Calvin leaned against the wall. His eyes were red, face fallen into despair.

"You all right, Father?" Rand asked.

Calvin only shook his head. "How do you do it? How do you face down evil like that over and over and feel nothing?"

"I definitely feel something."

Calvin looked as if he didn't believe him. Rand felt exhausted, hopeless, and empty, like he was on a treadmill that would never end. In a way, he was. Removing Karax from St. Mary's was well and good, but there would always be another demon, another haunting, another victim. He supposed the feelings he had after every encounter were locked away deep inside him, a coping mechanism that kept him stoic and steadfast for the next battle. Because if he wasn't there to be strong, who else would be?

"Thank you for saving her," Calvin said. "You did what I could not."

"I couldn't have done it without you," Rand said. The man's prayers had helped rebuff the demon, keeping it from becoming so much worse.

Calvin didn't seem to believe that either. He looked like he needed a long vacation. Or maybe a stiff drink. Possibly both. "I hope to see you again, Rand. But I pray it will be under different circumstances."

Rand left him and went into the ICU visitor area, where Nick, Maria, and the others had weathered the storm. It was empty except for Katie.

She looked at him from the couch when he came in. "How is everyone?"

"Happy. Like a family again."

"I'm sorry I never told you," she said. "That wasn't fair to you."

Rand sat next to her and set his bag by his feet. "It's okay."

But he wasn't sure he believed those words. Thoughts of a son came into his mind again. For so long, Libby had been his only family. But after knowing there had been the possibility for one more, the idea had latched onto him. Taken root and given him a desire he didn't know he had.

A second child.

But it was a dream he could never claim. It would not be fair to expose another child to the life he lived.

"I hate that thing for bringing it up," Katie said. "I should have known it would."

Demons were not bound by time or place. They knew everything about everyone, and they would use it against you if they felt threatened.

"I should leave," Katie said.

"I'll bring you home."

"No. Your daughter and girlfriend are waiting for you in the hall. Go with them."

He found Libby and Rachel where Katie had said they would be, surrounded by maintenance men going in and out of the ICU with equipment and tools. They both wrapped him in a tight hug.

"Are you okay?" Rachel asked. "I was so worried. Those horrible sounds coming from there…"

"Everything is fine. It's over."

"And Georgia?" Libby asked.

"She's back to normal," Rand said.

"Did you see it? The demon?"

Rand put his arm around her daughter's shoulder. "You know there's no point in talking about it now."

Out of the corner of his eye, Rand spotted a man among the working maintenance crew. He stood out because he was standing still against the wall while all the others were moving around him. Rand got the feeling he was being watched, but couldn't quite see the man's face from the cap pulled low over his eyes.

"Should we go now?" Rachel asked, breaking his concentration.

"Yeah."

"Can I say bye to Georgia?" Libby asked.

"She's with her family. Leave them be for now."

They walked toward the door but halted when Rand stopped short. "I forgot my bag. I'll run and get it real quick."

Rand returned to the ICU visitor area. It was empty now—Katie had gone. He looked beside the couch where he knew he'd left his bag when he'd spoken with her, but it wasn't there.

Someone must have picked it up.

The security station where the visitors signed in was unattended. He checked behind the desk to see if the guard had put it there, but it wasn't there either.

The elevator on the side of the waiting room dinged. The door slid open and no one was inside. However, Rand's bag was propped against the wall of the elevator, as if placed there.

What the hell?

The doors should have closed long before then, but they remained open. It was the service elevator, so it was larger than a normal one—big enough to carry ladders, machines, and other equipment around the hospital. Rand figured it was being used by the repairmen in the ICU.

He walked inside and to the far wall of the elevator, then snatched up his bag. As soon as he touched it, the elevator dinged again, and the doors began to close.

Rand rushed to stick his hand between them so it would open again, but the door ignored him, sliding closed and threatening to crush him. He moved it out of the way just in time.

He pressed the buttons on the control panel, but none

of them responded. Next, he tried the red help button, but it did not light up or activate.

Rand's pulse quickened. He gripped the handle on his bag. *I've taken the bait and fallen into a trap.*

He felt the hairs rise on the back of his neck. And he knew that whatever had brought him there was behind him.

He turned. The man he'd spotted earlier among the maintenance crew had appeared out of thin air.

But it was his face that stood out. He resembled a person, but his flesh seemed stretched too tight and was a light shade of blue. The eyes were small and completely filled with black.

Randolph.

He heard the demon's voice in his head, communicating telepathically. His mouth did not move.

And Rand knew who he was.

"Shindael."

You are well known where I come from. The demon's words were a whisper in Rand's mind, almost soothing. But also threatening. *You have met and bested many of my servants.*

Rand swallowed hard. "What do you want?"

I want you. And I will have you.

Shindael glared at Rand through his tiny black eyes. Rand wondered how many demons he'd faced in the past that had served Shindael directly.

Deep down, he'd always known that the more powerful demons would eventually come for him. Rand figured casting Karax out of Georgia was the final straw, and now Shindael was here.

I vow to torment you until the day you die. I vow to destroy

your family. I vow to end your life. I will send all the angels of
hell after you until both your body and soul are broken.

Those words settled into Rand's mind, and he knew he would never forget them. He also understood it was true. Shindael would keep his word.

That declaration cemented the rest of his life as a never-ending battle with the demonic. Like a diagnosis of a terminal illness, it filled him with fear. Even regret—he'd played with fire too many times and had finally gotten burned. There was no going back. But Rand was determined to stay strong in the presence of his nemesis.

"I guess I'll be seeing you again," he said.

Rand wasn't sure, but he thought there was a shadow of a smile on Shindael's face. Surely he knew how hard Rand was fighting to maintain his composure.

The elevator dinged and the door opened behind him. Rand turned his back on Shindael and left.

When he got down the hall, and then looked over his shoulder, the demon had disappeared.

39

R and woke at six o'clock the next morning when Rachel got up for work. She showered in his bathroom, did her makeup, and dressed quietly.

"You all right?" Rand asked her as she headed for the door. He propped himself up on his elbow in bed.

"Yeah," she said. "Didn't sleep that well." She left without another word.

Rand frowned. Neither had he. All the events from the hospital the night before still lingered in his mind. That, and Shindael's threat.

He threw off the covers and pulled on a pair of sweatpants before he went to the kitchen. He found Libby sitting at the table. She had put on a pot of coffee, and the aroma drifted through the air.

"What's up with Rachel?" Libby asked. "She walked by, but didn't say much."

"She said she didn't sleep well last night."

"Ah." Libby eyed him for a few moments. "You don't look that great either. Did you two have a fight?"

"I just woke up, Libby. Of course I don't look great."

"No. It's not that. You seem… worried."

Rand busied himself at the refrigerator so he didn't have to make eye contact with his daughter. Sometimes it freaked him out how well she could read him.

"Dad? Is everything actually over? With the thing?"

"Yes, it's over."

"Then why—"

"I don't know," he said, more terse than he meant to. "Maybe I'm just tired."

Libby didn't seem to buy his answer. "Fine. Go back to bed, then. I'm heading to school."

She swiped a banana and a granola bar from the counter and hustled out the front door, returning his coldness.

After she left, the house was silent and still. Too quiet. Rand had to find a way to occupy himself, to take his mind away.

Sixteen days had passed since Karax had told Georgia when she was going to die.

It was now the seventeenth day, and Rand knew it would be one of the longest of his life.

He felt helpless and hopeless. Like an inmate sitting on death row waiting for the final hour. If Georgia was meant to succumb to her illness on the seventeenth day, there was nothing he could do to change her fate.

At least what I did was not in vain, he told himself. *If it does happen, I still gave her peace for her last day on Earth.*

Although the thoughts did little to comfort him.

Around six in the evening, he heard a car pull up in

front of his house. When he drew the curtain aside, he saw it was Rachel. Odd. She hadn't mentioned she was coming back after work.

He opened the door as she walked across the yard. When Rand saw the look on her face, he knew something was wrong.

He had seen that expression many times before.

"You all right?" Rachel asked. "Have you left the house today?"

"You didn't say you were coming over."

"I know," she said. "I was on the way to the store. Thought I would stop by for a minute."

It was a beautiful fall evening and the air chilled him. The sun was setting over the trees. The two of them stood rigid, and Rand waited.

"I wanted to talk to you," Rachel said, suddenly very serious.

Rand set his jaw. "Go ahead." Although he already knew what was coming.

Rachel took a moment to form her thoughts. "I'm sorry, but I don't think I can do this."

He'd heard many break-up lines in his life. That one in particular seemed to be the most popular.

"It's my work," Rand said. Not a question.

"Yes. I know you help lots of people with what you do, but it's just too much for me, especially this past week. All that weird and crazy stuff happening. I can't take it."

"I'm sorry it affected you like that," Rand said. "It's the nature of the job, and these things happen." Still, that didn't make it okay for her to be collateral damage.

Rand remembered Shindael's promise—how the rest of his life would be a war with hell that would affect everyone he cared about. The safest thing for Rachel would be if they stopped seeing each other altogether.

"It's just too much for me," Rachel said. "I know I can't ask you to stop doing it."

Rand swallowed a hard lump in his throat. *She's right. She can't.* Even if he wanted to give it all up, it was too late for that. Shindael had already made that clear.

Rand reached out and stroked her arm, and she leaned into his touch. "I get it. This is not for everyone. If you feel unsafe with me, then there's no other way. You have to take care of yourself first."

"So you're not mad?"

"Of course not. Sad, definitely. I care about you a lot. But if what I do is too much, then it's best for us to head our separate ways."

Rachel looked like she might cry. It was a shame he was so accustomed to the women he cared about leaving him because of the supernatural monsters that attacked him. There was a time when women ending relationships with him had upset him, but he'd become numb to it long ago. Ever since Tessa had left him, no other breakup had had quite the impact. Honestly, that worried Rand. His life of fighting the demonic was eroding the things that made him human.

Rand walked Rachel back to her car. As she got in and drove away, he wished her the best. She deserved to find a normal, great man who wasn't followed around by evil spirits wreaking acts of terror.

In a different life, he could have given that to her.

For a moment, he imagined what it would be like if he gave it up. A new life, settled down alongside someone, without the fear of the demonic.

But people needed him. They depended on him. There would always be another case around the corner.

And when he remembered Shindael's words, he knew that wasn't even an option anymore. So he didn't dwell on the fantasy for too long.

Rachel drove away. He stood at the edge of his yard and watched her turn out of the neighborhood.

On top of his feelings of dread and uncertainty, he now felt worse. *Not her fault. She had no idea that today was significant.* The only person he had told about the seventeen days was Katie.

When he went back inside, he had a text from her, asking if he'd heard any news.

Not yet.

She responded a minute later.

I've been praying.

Rand knew he should have been as well, but was also aware it wouldn't change anything.

He forced himself to get into bed at ten o'clock. He called Libby before he turned his lamp off. She was staying with her mom, and they chatted for a bit.

"Oh my God. She broke up with you?"

"Yeah."

"Really? I thought she could handle you for the long haul."

"Apparently not."

"I'm sorry, Dad. Are you all right? Do I need to come over there?"

"I'm used to it."

"That isn't a good thing."

"I'll live."

They said goodnight and hung up. Libby hadn't brought up Georgia.

That's good. She would have mentioned something if she had heard.

Rand tossed and turned all night, drifting in and out. When he finally managed to fall asleep, Shindael's face filled his dreams, scaring him awake again.

Around seven in the morning, he trudged out of bed and into the living room.

Day eighteen. If she was meant to go, she'd be dead now.

That was why he'd gotten his black suit altered and dry-cleaned before Tessa's engagement party—so he'd have it in the event of an unexpected funeral.

He thumbed his cell phone, debating on whether or not to call Nick Collins. He would say he was calling to check on Georgia and see how she was doing after her ordeal. Then he would know for sure. No more wondering.

But he couldn't bring himself to do it.

Not yet.

His heart was heavy, sitting like a stone in his chest. If the worst had happened, he just wasn't ready to hear it.

That day, he only had morning classes. So, he headed over to campus, did his thing, and then ducked out after the lessons were over so he wouldn't get held up by anyone.

When he got home, Libby's car was in the driveway. It wasn't her day to stay with him, and even though he and Tessa didn't adhere to a strict schedule with her, Libby usually told him when she was planning to come over.

He found her lying on the couch. "What are you doing here?"

"Nice to see you, too."

"That's not what I mean. Normally you give a heads-up. I don't think I have any food here."

"I figured you'd want company after what Rachel did."

"No need," he said, setting his bag on the floor beside the door. He dropped his car keys on the nearby table.

"But I also brought you a gift," Libby said, sitting up on the couch.

"I don't want gifts, either. You know how I am. I'll get over it after six or seven beers."

He walked toward the kitchen to grab the first of those beers from the fridge, and then a figure caught the corner of his eye, startling him.

It was her.

Georgia.

She stood off to the side of his kitchen, out of sight from where he'd come through the front door.

"I was supposed to scare you. Did it work?"

As he stared at her, an oxygen cannula dangling from her nose, he couldn't help but break into a huge smile. He almost started crying. He walked up to her and wrapped her in a tight hug.

Georgia's body was rigid and awkward. "Uh. What did I do to deserve this?"

"You're still here."

"What is that supposed to mean?"

Rand let her go and looked down at her. She gave him a curious, suspicious look, but it only made him laugh. "Nothing. It's just good to see you."

"You're not sick of me yet?"

Libby joined them in the kitchen. "She's your gift, by

the way." To Georgia, she said, "He never greets *me* like that."

"You must not bring enough demons into his life."

Day eighteen and she's still alive, Rand thought. His entire body lost the tension that had built up over the last twenty-four hours.

"Come on," he said. "This is a celebration. I'll cook something. What do you two want? I don't have any food so, Libby, you'll have to go to the store to get some stuff."

"What are we celebrating, exactly?" Libby asked. She and Georgia both gave him a weird look.

"We just are."

Beer forgotten, he pulled out his pots and pans to prep for dinner. Georgia Collins showing up in his house had made him happier than he'd been in a long time.

For now, at least, he could forget about Shindael and Karax and all the rest. They'd be back on his mind in the morning, for sure, but that evening, he was a free man.

People like Georgia were the reason he would never give it up—people who were helpless and confused, and had nowhere else to turn.

They were why he fought. They were why he lived. They were why he served.

—

Randolph Casey returns in The Perfect Possession, the **second book** in the Randolph Casey Horror Thriller series.

Visit Rockwell Scott's website to learn more and read a free sample.

www.rockwellscott.com/books

Join Rockwell Scott's Reader Group to receive bonus content and hear about new releases by visiting his website.

www.rockwellscott.com/free-book

As soon as you sign up, you'll also receive a FREE gift—a supernatural horror novella that is not available anywhere else. You'll be able to download the ebook directly to your e-reading device in seconds.

HEY THERE.

Thank you for spending your valuable time reading my book, and I hope you enjoyed it.

As you may know, reviews are one of the best ways readers can support their favorite authors. They help get the word out and convince potential readers to take a chance on me.

I would like to ask that you consider leaving a review wherever you purchased this book. I would be very grateful, and of course, it is always valuable to me to hear what my readers think of my work.

Thank you in advance to everyone who chooses to do so, and I hope to see you back in my pages soon.

Sincerely,

- Rockwell

ALSO BY ROCKWELL SCOTT

A Haunting in Silver Falls

A quiet town. A cursed statue. An ancient evil claiming its next victim...

Sixteen-year-old Kara Mills expects her summer in Silver Falls to be dull—spent in a small town she doesn't care for with an aunt she barely knows. But boredom quickly turns to dread when Aunt Adrienne brings home an eerie statue from a local thrift shop. What starts as a strange curiosity soon takes on a life of its own.

The statue vanishes and reappears in different places around the house, leaving Kara to question her own senses. While she assumes it's her aunt playing tricks, Adrienne, a deeply spiritual woman, insists that a powerful spirit resides within the statue—and she welcomes it.

At first, Kara is skeptical. She can only watch as her quirky aunt offers small gifts to the statue and talks to it as if it's listening. But as the days pass, Adrienne's fascination turns into obsession and devotion. She grows cold and distant toward Kara, her behavior more erratic—and dangerous.

Soon Kara can no longer deny that something is very wrong. Terrified and alone, she witnesses her aunt falling deeper under the influence of a dark force. As evil begins to pervade Adrienne's entire home, Kara must confront the truth behind the statue before it consumes them both. But the malevolent entity within won't let go without a fight—and the cost of saving Adrienne could be more than Kara is prepared to pay.

ALSO BY ROCKWELL SCOTT

A Haunting in Rose Grove

A malevolent entity. A violent haunting. A house with a bloody history. Jake Nolan left it all behind, but now he must return.

Jake has it all — a new home, an amazing girlfriend, and nearing a promotion at work. Best of all, he feels he's finally moved on from the horrors of his traumatic past. But when he learns that his estranged brother, Trevor, has moved back into their haunted childhood home, Jake knows his past is not quite finished with him yet.

Jake rushes to the old house in Rose Grove — a small town with a tragic history — to pull his brother from that dangerous place.

But it's too late. There, he finds Trevor trying to make contact with the spirit that tormented them years ago.

And Trevor refuses to leave. He is determined to cleanse the house and remove the entity. But the supernatural activity becomes too much to handle, and Jake knows they are both unprepared for the fight. Worse, the entity targets Daniel, Jake's young nephew, and wants to bring him harm. And when the intelligent haunting shows signs of demonic infestation, Jake realizes they aren't dealing with a mere ghost.

Jake attributes the evil spirit for driving his parents to an early grave. Now it wants to claim the rest of the family, and the only way Jake and Trevor will survive is to send the entity back to hell.

A Haunting in Rose Grove is a supernatural horror novel for readers who love stories about haunted houses and battles with the demonic — the truest form of evil that exists in our world.

ALSO BY ROCKWELL SCOTT

The Gravewatcher

Every night at 3 AM, he visits the graveyard and speaks to someone who isn't there.

Eleanor has created an ideal life for herself in New York City with a career that keeps her too busy, just as she likes it. But when she receives an anonymous message that her estranged brother Dennis is dead, her fast-paced routine grinds to a halt. She rushes to Finnick, Louisiana — the small, backward town where her brother lived and temporarily settles into his creepy, turn-of-the-century house until she can figure out how he died.

But that night, Eleanor spots a young boy in the cemetery behind Dennis's house, speaking to the gravestones. When she approaches him, Eleanor's interruption of the boy's ritual sets off a chain reaction of horror she could have never prepared for. The footsteps, the voices, and the shadowy apparitions are only the beginning.

Eleanor learns that the boy, Walter, is being oppressed by a demonic entity that compels him to visit the graveyard every night. She suspects Dennis also discovered this nightly ritual and tried to stop it, and that is why he died. Because there are others in Finnick who know about Walter's involvement with the evil spirit and want it to continue, and they will do whatever it takes to stop Eleanor from ruining their carefully laid plans. Now Eleanor must finish what her brother started — to rescue the boy from the clutches of hell before he loses his soul forever.

The Gravewatcher is a supernatural horror novel for readers who love stories about haunted houses, creepy graveyards, and battles with the demonic - the truest form of evil that exists in our world.

ABOUT THE AUTHOR

Rockwell Scott is an author of supernatural horror
fiction.

When not writing, he can be found working out, enjoying
beer and whiskey with friends, and traveling
internationally.

Feel free to get in touch!

Instagram
https://www.instagram.com/rockwellscottauthor/

Facebook
www.facebook.com/rockwellscottauthor

X
@rockwell_scott

www.rockwellscott.com

rockwellscottauthor@gmail.com

Printed in Great Britain
by Amazon